Quickly, and without having to be given specific orders as to what to do, the raiders spread out over the bridge. They drilled holes in the timbers and braces, put torpedoes into place, then lit the fuses.

Seconds later, the shock waves of the explosion moved across the field and hit Rindell, making his stomach shake. The fuses had been timed so that the blasts went together, starting as bursts of white-hot flame, then erupting black smoke from the points where the charges were laid. The underpinnings of the trestle were carried away by the torpedoes, but the superstructure remained intact for several more seconds. Then, slowly, the tracks began to sag and the ties started snapping, popping with a series of loud reports like pistol shots, until finally, with a resounding crash and a splash of water, the whole bridge collapsed into Shoal's Creek.

Rindell, even as he admired Colonel Tyreen's strategy, breathed a little prayer that his message had been delivered to Faraday, and the train diverted.

Other books in the Faraday Series

#1: IRON HORSE
#2: COLLISION COURSE

FARADAY #3

THE GOLD TRAIN

William Grant

TM BCI Created by the producers of Wagons West, Stagecoach, Badge, and White Indian.

Book Creations Inc., Canaan, NY · Lyle Kenyon Engel, Founder

LYNX BOOKS
New York

FARADAY #3: THE GOLD TRAIN

ISBN: 1-55802-183-3

First Printing/November 1988

Produced by Book Creations, Inc.
Founder: Lyle Kenyon Engel

This book is published by Lynx Books, a division of Lynx Communications, Inc., 41 Madison Avenue, New York, New York, 10010.

Printed in the United States of America

0 9 8 7 6 5 4 3 2 1

FARADAY #3

THE GOLD TRAIN

Chapter 1

THE *WESTERN FLYER*, ITS FOUR-BY-FOUR BALDWIN ENgine pulling a baggage car, three sleepers, and three day cars, was thirty hours out of Cincinnati when it pulled into Washington D.C. Behind it, wet tracks gleamed in the capital city's lights, the twin bands of silver disappearing in the distance. Ahead, a yellow light above a red one cut through the midnight darkness, signaling the engineer that the track before him had been switched to lead into the station.

As the train approached the depot yard, a figure dressed in black appeared on the top of the first car. With unsteady movement the dark form raced awkwardly along the length of the car, then leaped the gap to the next one, faltering a moment on the rain-slick surface before running on. The figure paused long enough to glance behind, and at that moment the silhouette of a second person appeared over the top of the first car. The first person jumped into action, leaping across to the third car as the other figure followed in pursuit.

Running along the top of a moving train was a difficult feat under the best of conditions, and with the rain the top of the cars were wet and slippery tonight. The cars shook and rocked as they passed over the uneven railbed of the depot yard, the train's diminished speed causing the slack between the cars to be taken up or increased by the couplers. Despite the glow of the moon, the night was dark enough to make the action of running along the car's tops even more difficult.

A gunshot rang out, but the whistle of the engine covered the sound so that the figure being pursued on top of the train could scarcely hear it. The flash from the pursuer's muzzle also went unnoticed, a momentary wink of light indistinguishable from the glowing embers and the flying sparks that whipped off the locomotive.

The runner made it to the last car and climbed down the ladder to the platform below. As the dark figure worked the latch of the door, the pursuer appeared over the top of the car, took careful aim, and fired a second shot. This time the bullet found its mark, though the victim's muffled cry of shock and pain was masked by the squeal of braking wheels. The runner slumped onto the platform and lay still. Quickly the pursuer climbed down the ladder, looked around for the sign of a witness, and then bent over to grasp the body. Lifting it by the underarms, the pursuer flung it over the side into the depot yard and reentered the train.

As the *Western Flyer* continued into the station, the lamps inside the cars were turned to bright so that the passengers could collect their belongings. The trip had been long and tiring, and most of the travelers would say that they were grateful it was over.

In the first car a young mother holding a baby in her arms reached for a hatbox on the overhead rack. She stretched as much as she could, but it was beyond her reach.

"Allow me," a bystander offered. A tall handsome

man with dark hair and mustache, he had just entered the car from the front. He smiled graciously at the lady and reached up to retrieve the hatbox.

"Why, thank you, sir. You are most kind."

"It's my pleasure, ma'am," the man said, touching the brim of his hat.

He was exceptionally well dressed in camel-colored trousers and a dark blue jacket. He had a pistol tucked in his belt, and when he saw the woman looking pointedly at it, he apologized. "I hope you aren't alarmed," he said. "I may look like a civilian, but in truth I'm a Union military officer, returning to duty from leave."

"Then I should be doubly grateful to you, sir, not only for helping me, but for serving our country in its hour of need."

"The graciousness of citizens such as yourself makes duty a privilege, ma'am, as I'm sure this young lieutenant will agree." He nodded toward a young army officer in uniform who had his arm in a sling.

"Yes, sir, I most heartily concur," the lieutenant said quickly.

The older man touched the brim of his hat again. "If you will excuse me?" he said. Then he smiled and moved through the car to exit at the other end.

"What a nice man," the woman said.

"Yes, ma'am, he was very courteous," the lieutenant agreed. With his good hand, he stroked a beard so light and sparse that it was nearly invisible. "But it's strange about that pistol."

"Oh, but he explained that he is an army officer returning to duty," the young mother replied as she shifted the bundled baby from one arm to the other.

"Yes, I heard him, ma'am, but I swear I smelled cordite, as if that pistol had just been fired."

"Just fired?" The young woman laughed. "That isn't very likely, is it, Lieutenant?"

The lieutenant smiled sheepishly. "No, ma'am, I guess it's not. I've been in so many battles, I guess everything smells like cordite."

* * *

An hour after the train had pulled into the station, a young Union guard was making his rounds of the depot yard. With his coat collar turned up, his hands thrust deep into his pockets, and his rifle slung over his shoulder, he picked his way over ties and damp rocks, negotiating the long circuit around the depot yard. When he reached the outer edge of the yard, he saw a black shadow beside the track. Fearing it was debris that might blow onto the rails and cause an accident, he quickened his step.

He was twenty-five yards away when he realized the shadow was not trash, but a person. He wondered if it was a drunk.

It took ten more yards before the young soldier was convinced that it was not a drunk. The form was too still and was lying in a grotesque position, its left leg unnaturally flung up toward the shoulder. The soldier stopped and took a shallow breath. Then he turned and hurried back to the station to get the switchman.

"Lord'a mercy," the switchman said as he rolled the body over. "Would you look at this? It's a woman."

The young guard leaned over the woman, her face illuminated by the lantern the switchman held. It was the body of a woman, but she was wearing men's clothing.

"What's she doin' out here?" the young soldier asked. "And why's she wearin' clothes like that?"

"I don't know," the switchman said, running his hands over the body. "Doesn't appear she was hit by the train."

"Maybe she fell off."

"Could be," the switchman said. "But here's somethin' else to ponder. This here woman's been shot."

"Shot?"

"In the back."

"She seems so young," the young soldier said sadly.

"Boy, there's been young folks dyin' for four years," the older man said.

"Yes, but she's a woman."

"Men ain't got a corner on dyin'. Women got to die too." He shouldered his rifle. "Reckon I'll walk back to the guard-shack an' tell the Corporal of the Guard what we found. Like as not, he'll want to send word to the police. This is more their concern than ours."

Though it did not rain again for the remainder of the night, clouds continued to gather so that the next morning dawned damp, overcast, and cold. Those who found it necessary to be outside bundled up. Streetcars moved up and down the city streets, trailing plumes of smoke from woodstoves burning at the rear.

In a third-floor office overlooking the corner of E and Tenth streets, where the tracks crossed, Matthew Faraday, founder and owner of the Faraday Security Service, sat at his desk reading an article in the *Washington Evening Star* dated April 5, 1864, under the headline "A Mystery":

> At one o'clock this morning, the body of a young woman was discovered lying alongside the tracks in the Baltimore and Ohio depot yard.
>
> The unidentified woman was shot in the back. She is believed to have been between twenty-five and thirty years of age, fair of hair and complexion, and with a face that could be described as comely, were it not disfigured by a fall on the rocks. The mystery is deepened by her being clothed in unusual attire, trousers and a coat, as if she had been disguising herself as a man.
>
> Thus far, the police have been unsuccessful in discovering the perpetrator of this evil deed. Anyone who might have information regarding this murder is requested to come to police headquarters forthwith to disclose same.

Matthew Faraday folded the paper, put it on his desk, and stood up. He had a sick sensation in the pit of his stomach. He did not want to say the words aloud—he did not even want to think them—but he had a feeling he knew the identity of the woman. He pulled a cigar from the humidor, lit it, then walked to the window. On this spring morning Washington was cloudy and damp, heralding the onset of the oppressive humidity that made the city all but uninhabitable in the summer. Even the official buildings designed in the Greek classical style looked dingy. The unpaved streets were muddy and dotted with horse droppings, and he saw a well-dressed woman picking her way gingerly between the mud puddles and manure, hurrying across Tenth to catch a trolley.

Staying at the window is not going to change things, Faraday told himself. If the dead woman was who he thought it was, he would have to face up to it sooner or later. With a sad sigh, he took his coat from the rack, and trudged down the stairs to catch the trolley downtown.

A few minutes later he was sitting beside the stove at the rear of a trolley car, headed toward the city morgue. He watched a soldier from the Seventh Ohio regiment attempting to make light conversation with a pretty young woman seated nearby. Faraday was thinking that the young woman was about twenty-three, Sarah Cunningham's age. It made him think back to when she had first approached him, exactly a year ago. . . .

"Miss Cunningham," he said, "while a certain sense of adventure is needed to be successful in a job such as I offer, one shouldn't lose sight of the danger inherent in this work."

Sarah laughed, tossing her blond hair back from her forehead. "You sound as if you're reading that out of a book, Mr. Faraday."

"I'm just trying to make you aware of the hazards," Matthew Faraday replied.

Sarah carefully composed her face into a more serious expression. "Mr. Faraday, I understand there are dangers involved, but I also know that you are doing work for the Union . . . important work. My brother died at Gettysburg last year. If I were a man, I would be in General Sheridan's cavalry."

"To avenge your brother's death?"

"No, it's not revenge I'm after. He was killed in a battle fought by men of honor on both sides. I don't think that kind of death demands vengeance. But I would like to carry on the work my brother started. He wasn't fighting for the glory and excitement of it, Mr. Faraday. He believed in the Union . . . and I believe in it. That's why I want to work for you."

Faraday smiled and reached out to take her hand. "Miss Cunningham," he said, "if that's really your attitude, then I would be proud to have you working for me."

And now Sarah Cunningham was missing, possibly dead.

Matthew Faraday, silver-haired and distinguished, looked like what he was, a successful businessman. But his business was not conducted from the overstuffed chair in his plush office. His was not an ordinary enterprise, involved with commerce or trade, but something of an entirely different nature. His detective agency was under contract to the major railroad lines.

The operation of the agency was now more important than it had ever been. With the Civil War raging and the railroads providing a vital link between the nation's capitol and the northern industrial cities, the railroads had become tempting targets for Southern rebels. Most dangerous were rebels from border states, where Southern sentiment burned.

Matthew Faraday was hired to prevent any such attack, and in the process he was also able to provide another important service to his country. Since he had clients throughout the North and South and agents involved in clandestine activities, he was thrust into the position of heading a national intelligence gathering agency.

Sarah Cunningham had turned out to be one of the Faraday Security Service's best agents. Young and beautiful, she looked so innocent that she could appear anywhere without arousing suspicion. Several times over the last six months she had transmitted valuable information. And three days ago, when she had sent her last telegram informing Matthew that she would be returning on the *Western Flyer*, she had signaled that she had urgent information. She had also included a code word indicating that her cover might have been compromised and that it was too dangerous for her to remain in the field.

It was the note of concern in that telegram and her not showing up on last night's train that made Matthew Faraday fear the worst.

The city morgue was located behind the midtown precinct station. Faraday walked up the concrete steps to the front door, pushed it open, and stepped inside. He followed the hallway to a large, stark-white receiving room. On the wall hung a calendar with the year, 1864, printed in bold black type just below a picture of a farm. On the sheet below was the month, April, with every day except today's date, the fifth, carefully crossed out. Beside the calendar was a large, bold-faced clock. The time was three-fifteen.

The desk sergeant, a large, red-haired, ruddy man, was writing in a ledger. When Faraday stopped in front of the desk, the sergeant looked up.

"Aye . . . and what can I be doin' for you this fine day, Mr. Faraday? Sergeant O'Rourke at your service, sir."

Though the Washington police knew Matthew Faraday, they were unaware of his deep involvement in espionage activities and would not suspect the young woman whose identity was unknown to be one of Faraday's agents.

"Sergeant, I read an article in today's paper about a young lady in your morgue. Is she still unidentified?"

"Aye. The lass is still with us. Would you be knowin' her?"

"I don't know," Faraday said. "I might."

"'Tis hopin', I am, that she's not one of your loved

ones," O'Rourke said. "Though we would like to identify her."

"Do you know anything about her?"

"Nothing, sir. 'Tis a shame such a bonnie lass had to die at such a tender age. But then there's many a lad keepin' an untimely appointment with his Maker these days."

"May I see her?"

"Aye, come along. You're welcome to view the body"—the red-haired sergeant shook his head—"though I must tell you that what was once a lovely face is now a sight that'll wrench your heart."

Faraday followed the policeman through the double doors and down a long hall and into another room at the back of the building. The air was noticeably colder here, and Faraday saw the blocks of ice stored on special shelves to keep the temperature down. Half a dozen tables stood in the middle of the room, four of them holding shrouded bodies.

"Which one is she?"

"This one," O'Rourke said, pointing to the table with the smallest body.

"Are the others known to you?"

"Aye, two are hoodlums, shot down by our own police force last night. The other is a man who died in jail and is waitin' to be taken to the potter's field." He pulled back the sheet on the fourth body. "Here she is, Mr. Faraday. Would you be knowin' her, sir?" he asked gently.

Faraday looked at the young woman's face. Bruised and cut, it was twisted out of shape by the slackness of death. She made a pitiful sight, but she was unmistakably Sarah.

"I know her," Faraday said quietly. "Her name is Sarah Cunningham."

The policeman rearranged the sheet over the body and looked at Faraday. "'Tis the saddest part of my job, showin' these poor souls to their loved ones. Are you all right?"

"I am, thank you."

"Come along, then. There's no point breakin' your heart in here."

Faraday looked back once, then followed the sergeant from the morgue.

"If you'd be so kind as to give me the pertinent facts, I'll be fillin' out the papers on the wee lass."

As they walked back to the receiving room, Faraday saw two policemen pushing a sullen prisoner toward one of the holding cells. A bruise over his left eye showed that he had not come peaceably.

When they reached the receiving room, O'Rourke took out a printed form and began filling in the blanks.

"You say the girl's name was Sarah Cunningham?"

"That is correct."

"Are you related to her?"

"I'm her first cousin," Faraday said. For security reasons, he thought it was best to lie about their relationship. The only way he could discharge his responsibility to Sarah now was to pose as a relative. Since he routinely took a family interest in his agents, he did not feel he was stretching the truth too much. It would certainly be less painful for Sarah's family if he handled everything himself. Otherwise, they would be forced to endure a sad and difficult trip from New York.

At a local funeral home, he arranged for Sarah's body to be prepared and shipped home. He gave the undertaker's wife money to buy a dress, and he asked that the clothes Sarah was wearing be turned over to him.

"I wouldn't want the bereaved family to see those," he said. "It would only add embarrassment to their grief."

"Yes," the undertaker's wife said, thinking that no decent woman would wear men's clothing . . . especially not in death.

An hour later, she informed Faraday that he could view the body. Sarah had been properly dressed, the bruises on her face covered by the undertaker's artifice. The wife stood by, beaming proudly at the handiwork. "Doesn't she look lovely and lifelike?" she asked.

"Yes," Faraday said, because it was easier to agree than to admit that the waxen form did not look at all lifelike to him. At least, he told himself, it did not look like Sarah Cunningham. Where was the joy, the excitement, the warmth?

"Here are the clothes she was wearing," the woman said, handing him a wrapped parcel.

Faraday took the parcel, thanked her, and waited for the buckboard that was to transport the coffin to the railroad station. Then he watched as the coffin was placed in the baggage car of the New York Special, telling himself that Sarah Cunningham was taking her last train ride home.

Later, when he returned to his apartment, Faraday made a thorough examination of the clothes Sarah had been wearing. He knew the pockets would be empty; the police had given him the contents—three dollars in silver, the stub of a pencil, and a piece of string. In the cuffs of the pants, he found sand and small bits of grass, nothing of any help. But in the lining of the jacket, he found a piece of paper with writing on it.

"Sarah, you left something for me," he said with quiet excitement. "Wherever you are, girl, bless your heart."

He smoothed out the paper and read the message: *104FNKCSQZHM.*

The odd sequence of numbers and letters made no sense to anyone but Faraday. The code was his own design. If the message was written during the first week of the month, each letter would be moved back one space in the alphabet. If it was written during the second week, the letters were moved two spaces, three spaces for the third, four for the fourth. At the end of the alphabet, the *Z* moved back one space, becoming an *A*. The messages were written without spaces between the words, unless a space was absolutely necessary to avoid misinterpretation. Numbers preceding the text were reversed to give the date the message was written.

In the case of Sarah's message, the numerals 104 were reversed to indicate April first. Since the first was during the first week of the month, Faraday knew to move the letters back one space to decode the message.

It took him only a moment. "Gold train," he read. Then he shook his head. He had no idea what it meant.

Chapter 2

On the Dalton Road a few miles outside Resaca, Georgia, stood a large plantation manor surrounded by beautifully landscaped grounds. Stately sweet gum and magnolia trees that shaded the drive in the heat of summer were in full bloom, and the early morning mist clung to the roses and honeysuckle twined thickly about the doric columns that supported the grand veranda. Long, muslin curtains billowed in the soft breeze, a pleasant flower-scented breath of spring.

Oddly, a battalion of cavalry was camped on the same well-kept parcel of land. The cavalrymen began to stir, and soon smoke drifted from their breakfast fires, the aroma of salt pork and coffee invading the manor house and filling the woods.

A soldier, naked from the waist up, bent over a washbasin attending to his morning ablutions. With soap on his face and in his eyes, he reached for a towel, which another soldier playfully jerked away from him.

"Ebenezer!" the first soldier howled. "Ebenezer, is that you?"

"You want this towel, Booker?" Ebenezer taunted,

dancing around the soldier with the soap-covered face.

"Ebenezer, you is the most aggravatin' critter in all of Tyreen's cavalry . . . even in this whole Confederate Army!"

Ebenezer played the game a moment longer, then handed the towel back to Booker. The soldier wiped his face, opened his eyes, and looked up at the enormous manor of the plantation, which was called Trailback. An officer astride a big chestnut horse was just riding up the circular path in front of the stately mansion. Arriving at the front stairway, he dismounted, returned the salute of the guard, and hurried up the stairs to enter the front door.

Booker, towel in hand, pointed at the officer. "That there is the meanest son of a bitch ever to draw a breath," he said.

"Chambers?"

"Blackwell Woodson Chambers," Booker corrected, spitting disparagingly on the ground.

"You knew him before the war, didn't you?"

"Yea, I knew him. 'Course, he was a big plantation owner then. He never had nothin' to do with folks like us who hadn't but forty acres and a mule."

"Still, he could'a paid his way outta the war," Ebenezer said. "Leastwise, you got to give him credit for coming in."

"It don't do our side no good to have people like him wearin' the gray."

Booker slipped on his tunic. Well mended and clean from the previous night's washing, it nevertheless showed the effects of four years of war. The gray had faded considerably, and the gold cuffs with their three stripes of rank had faded. It no longer looked anything like the proud uniform of a Confederate soldier.

"There's probably Yankee soldiers saying the same thing 'bout some of their officers," Ebenezer suggested.

"Could be," Booker replied. "But they're up there, and we're down here with Tyreen's Raiders, the best train busters in the Confederacy! I say a prayer ever'night to keep Colonel Tyreen alive, so Blackie Chambers don't ever get command."

"Cap'n Rindell's all right," Ebenezer said.

"Cap'n Rindell ain't the executive officer. Major Chambers is." Booker tucked his shirt into his belt, strapped on his pistol, and put on his cap. "Come on. Let's go get our grits."

"Umm, taste those pancakes," one of the officers on Tyreen's staff said, shoving a forkful into his mouth. "I don't know when I've had anything so good. Sir, you better eat 'em while they're hot."

"Later," Lieutenant Colonel Jebediah Tyreen said. He was standing by a large wall map, his tall, slender frame striking an impressive pose as he stroked his blond chin whiskers with his left hand—rather, with the hook that had served as his left hand since the battle of Shiloh. The map was a large-scale drawing of the United States east of the Mississippi River.

Captain Michael Rindell, Tyreen's adjutant, stood behind him. In his late twenties, Rindell was just under six feet tall, two inches shorter than Tyreen, but his shoulders were so broad and his arms so powerful that no one thought of him as small. Both men looked up when the tall, dark-haired form of Major Chambers loomed in the doorway.

"Major Chambers," Tyreen said. "You're just in time for breakfast. Lieutenant Dobbins was just singing the praises of the pancakes."

"Thank you, Colonel, but I've already had my breakfast. I'll have some coffee, though." Chambers smiled broadly, causing the disfiguring scar on his right cheek to change shape. Without the scar, he could have been called a handsome man. Rubbing his hands together enthusiastically, he stepped over to the table.

"You look like the cat that swallowed the canary," Tyreen said.

"Yes, sir, well, I guess I do. I got some news . . . I got some news that's gonna knock your hat off."

"Let's hear it, man, let's hear it!"

"I know where we can get some gold," Chambers said, pouring the hot coffee into a cup. "A lot of gold . . . more gold than any of us ever seen before."

"And how much is that?" Tyreen said skeptically.

"One million dollars in bullion."

"One million dollars?" Lieutenant Dobbins gasped.

"That's right, Lieutenant," Chambers replied.

"You're right, Blackie, that is more money than any of us have ever seen," Tyreen said, walking over to the table. "Where is this treasure supposed to be?"

"It's in Washington right now," Chambers said. "But it'll be coming south soon. The Yankees are sending it by special train." He smiled even more broadly and pointed to his chest. "And I know the route of travel."

"One million dollars?" the young lieutenant said again. He was so stunned by the amount of money mentioned that he had quit eating.

"One million dollars," Chambers repeated.

Tyreen's blue eyes shone brightly. "Do you gentlemen know what we could do with a million dollars?"

"We could buy this plantation and nine more just like it," Chambers said.

"How could we do that?" Rindell asked, speaking for the first time. "It wouldn't be our money, now would it?"

"No, no, of course not," Chambers said quickly. "I was just making an observation, that's all."

"Well, I'm not just making an observation, gentlemen," Tyreen said. "With that money we could buy enough weapons, ammunition, food, and clothing to turn the tide of battle. This could be what we've been waiting for . . . praying for." He stepped over to the wall map, picked up a pen, and turned to Chambers. "Where is this train going, and how can we get our hands on it?"

"Well, sir, it'll be leaving Washington in a few days, on the eighth, heading north toward Baltimore, west across Maryland, and on across traitors' Virginia."

"You mean West Virginia, don't you?" Rindell asked.

"There's no such place," Chambers growled. "There's only one Virginia. Part of it is loyal, and part of it is treasonous."

"I guess the folks in West Virginia figure they're the loyal ones," Rindell said.

"Sometimes, Captain, I don't think you know who's loyal and who isn't," Chambers snarled.

"Gentlemen, gentlemen, we have more important things to do than to quarrel among ourselves. Go on, Blackie." Tyreen had traced the train's path as Chambers had given it, and now he turned back to the map and lifted the pen. "You were describing the route."

"Yes, sir," Chambers continued. "The train'll be cutting 'cross Ohio to Cincinnati, then on to Louisville, and Nashville."

"The eighth is Friday," Tyreen said as he plotted the train's course. "That doesn't leave us much time to prepare. You're absolutely certain about this information?"

"Yes, sir. I told you I have a contact in Washington. He had a close call getting hold of this for us. . . . He even had to kill a Yankee agent who was getting too close."

"Nasty business, spying," Tyreen said, stroking his chin with the hook. "I prefer to fight my wars on the battlefield, where there are men of honor."

"Ha. It's men of honor that's got us on our knees now. All the West Point officers that come over to fight for the South, so full of duty, honor, country." He said the three words with scorn, then continued. "They forgot the most important thing is winning."

"You haven't forgotten, have you, Major, that I am a West Point officer?"

"Well, of course, sir, I didn't mean you," Chambers stammered.

"Victory without honor is no victory at all," Tyreen said sternly.

"It's better than losing," Chambers replied.

"I wonder."

Chambers cleared his throat. "Well, if you'll excuse me, sir, I got some things need doing."

"Go right ahead," Tyreen said. "And, Major, you did well to bring us that information."

"Thank you, sir." Chambers saluted sharply, then left the house.

"Mike," Tyreen said, "come out onto the front porch with me for a few minutes."

"All right, sir."

The two officers stepped through the French doors onto the veranda of Trailback, then walked to the railing and looked out over the rolling countryside. Here and there patches of red dirt—fields that had recently been plowed and planted—broke the lush green of the hillsides. The two men stood in silence, the forty-five-year-old colonel because he was reflective, Rindell, because he was the junior of the two.

"Did you ever come here before the war?" Tyreen finally asked. The light had caught the red-gold highlights in his hair.

"Do you mean to Resaca, sir?"

"No. I mean here, at Trailback."

"No, sir, I can't say as I did."

Still peering at the distant hills, Tyreen shook his head and said quietly, "I was here in fifty-nine. For as far as you could see, the fields were under cultivation . . . cotton, peanuts, corn, melons. There were more than two hundred darkies here then. You could hear them singing in the fields. . . . I never heard anything as beautiful. Marcus Culpepper was still alive then, and he used to give the most wonderful barbecues. You could smell the pork cooking over open pits, hear the children laughing and playing, see the beautiful young women and their beaux standing under the trees, strolling through the flower gardens. . . ." Tyreen's voice trailed off, and he was silent for a moment.

"Over there," he went on. "See, where that twelve-pounder cannon is in place? Once a charming gazebo stood on that spot. And down there . . . near the rifle pits? A bed of azalea."

Another long moment of silence passed, and then

Tyreen reached up to pinch the bridge of his nose with his good hand.

"And now," he said, speaking more quietly than before, "Marcus Culpepper and his two sons are dead. Mrs. Culpepper is in Savannah, an invalid living with her daughter. Trailback lies deserted, and the only fields under cultivation are those planted by neighbors or squatters."

"It's a sad sight," Rindell agreed.

"Mike, is Chambers right? Have men like me, men who prize honor above all else, caused the South to lose this war?"

Mike Rindell looked at the colonel and saw the tortured uncertainty in his eyes. Then he responded, "If the South does lose this war, Colonel, it will rebuild. And when it does, it will need men of honor more than ever."

Tyreen turned around and leaned his back against the railing. Crossing his arms and looking down, he said gravely, "I speak of honor, though I may be guilty of the greatest violation possible. I took an oath on the plains of West Point. I swore fidelity to duty, honor, and country. And for eighteen years, I was loyal to that oath. Then this accursed war forced me to choose between my state and the nation." Gazing at the porch floor, he shook his head again. "Only God knows if I made the right decision."

"I don't think God will pass judgment on you," Rindell said. "I'm certain that there are men of great conscience on both sides . . . men fighting for the North with the same dedication to honor as you feel for the South."

"And you, Mike. What do you believe?"

Rindell looked out across the lawn, studying a couple of privates who were busy splitting wood. Finally he sighed and turned toward his colonel.

"Sir, I believe there is no problem in doing what is right," he said. "The problem is in knowing what is right."

Tyreen chuckled. "I can't argue with that," he said,

turning to the younger man. "But Blackie might. He's always so sure of what's right."

"Such absolute certainty does make life easier," Rindell said sarcastically.

The expression on Tyreen's face grew serious. "Mike, look out for Chambers. . . . He doesn't like you, you know."

Rindell smiled. "Fortunately, sir, I don't have to please him. You're my commander."

"But if something should happen to me . . ."

"It's in my best interest to see that it doesn't."

Tyreen laughed. "Well, now, that's true. Maybe I'll just see what I can do about holding you to your promise. What do you say we go inside to plan how and where to stop this gold train?"

"All right."

As the two men walked across the veranda to the door, the colonel remarked, "One million dollars . . . Can you imagine the difference one million dollars would make to us now?"

They returned to the map, and Mike Rindell began studying the area north of Nashville.

"Colonel, I know the Louisville and Nashville Railroad pretty well. Look here, almost exactly halfway between Fountain Head and Gallatin is South Tunnel. The approaches to the tunnel are well concealed by the hills, making it an excellent place to stop the train."

"Yes, I agree," Tyreen said reflectively. After a few moments, he added, "Mike, I'm putting you in charge of making the plans."

Smiling at the colonel, Rindell said, "I'll do my best, sir." But as the young captain saluted, pivoted, and returned to the dining room to begin his work, he had many conflicting feelings about his assignment.

For the rest of the morning, Captain Rindell made plans for the attack. Spreading maps and charts on the dining room table, he located the routes of approach and considered the positioning of lookouts, determining how many men and how much equipment would be needed.

Shortly after noon the colonel entered the room, and Rindell pushed the papers to one side.

"Colonel Tyreen, I have to send a telegram," he said. "I have a friend in Richmond who used to work on that railroad. He'll have the answer to a few of my questions."

"Very well," Tyreen said. "I believe the line is through to Resaca. It shouldn't take you long to ride there."

When Rindell reached the barn to saddle his horse for the ride to Resaca, he found Booker and Ebenezer inside, brushing down their animals.

"Cap'n, is it true what we been hearin'?" Booker asked. "Are we really goin' after a train that's carryin' a million dollars?"

Rindell frowned. "Where'd you hear that?"

"It's bein' told all over the camp," Booker said.

Rindell took his saddle down and threw it on the back of his horse. "If too many people get to talking about it, we might as well put it in all the papers," he said. "Don't you think we might want to keep an operation like this secret?"

"Hell, Cap'n, we're the train busters," Booker said proudly. "If the Yankees is really plannin' on sendin' a million dollars on a train, they got to know Tyreen's Raiders are goin' to make a try for it. We've tore up more bridges, ripped out more track, and busted more engines than any other outfit in this whole war. I reckon this is just another train, except for all the money it's carryin'."

Cinching his saddle down, Rindell looked at Booker and Ebenezer. "We might be going after it, and we might not," he said. "I'm not saying one way or the other. But if you want some advice, you'll quit talking about it . . . and you'll get ready for a long ride."

"Yes, sir!" Booker replied, smiling broadly. "Man

oh man . . . I just want a chance to see that much money one time in my life."

"And Sergeant?" Rindell said.

"Yes, sir?"

"You'd better check all the men, make certain their horses are well shod and ready to ride. . . . Where's the lieutenant?"

"The lieutenant took his platoon out for some mounted drill a hour or so ago. But you can count on me, Cap'n. I'll check the horses that's in the camp now, and when the lieutenant gets back, I'll check the others."

"Good," Rindell said.

Swinging into the saddle, the captain rode away from the barn and down the road leading from the plantation to Resaca. As his horse found its pace, Rindell began to think about his commanding officer. Jebediah Tyreen was a man of skill and daring, as well as a man of honor. Rindell had not been with him during the battle of Shiloh, but he had heard of Tyreen's performance there. A Yankee cannon ball had taken off his left hand, leaving nothing but a bleeding stump. Tyreen had cauterized his own wound, tied a bandage around it, and then rallied his men to turn back a Union charge.

The loss of his hand had not slowed Tyreen down at all. His cavalry battalion, called Tyreen's Raiders, was everything Booker had boasted it was. As far as the railroads were concerned, Tyreen's Raiders were the most feared unit in the South. Mike Rindell knew they deserved the name "railroad busters," and the reputation.

It was the almost-mystical ability of Tyreen's Raiders to be in the right place at the right time that had caused Rindell to get himself assigned to the battalion. Using a connection in Richmond, he had gotten a commission. Now, as a captain in the Confederate Army and planning officer for Tyreen's Raiders, he was right in the middle of the greatest threat to the Union railroads.

And he was also in the greatest position to serve his boss, Matthew Faraday.

Mike Rindell was not a spy in the traditional sense. He was not a soldier of the opposing army acting behind the lines, nor was he working for the opposing government, transmitting information back to his superiors. But he was a spy, nonetheless. His loyalty and his mission were pledged to Matthew Faraday, not the Confederate Army—and not to Lieutenant Colonel Jebediah Tyreen.

That part of it troubled Rindell, because he genuinely liked Colonel Tyreen. Tyreen was the kind of man anyone would be proud to call friend, and yet Rindell knew that if Tyreen ever discovered what was really going on, the fate of the traitor in a Confederate uniform would be sealed. Friendship aside, Tyreen would have no qualms about trying Rindell in a court martial, sentencing him to death, and personally affixing the noose around his neck. And there were others in the Confederate Army whom Rindell liked . . . Sergeant Booker, Private Ebenezer Scruggs. He did not particularly care for Blackwell Chambers, because from the first Chambers had seemed jealous of Rindell, as if Tyreen might promote Rindell over him. Rindell had decided that Chambers was a generally disagreeable man . . . but he did feel badly about the others.

The young Faraday agent was about to cross a small stream when he heard a low rumble like the roll of kettledrums. He immediately recognized the sound of hoofbeats, many hoofbeats. Guiding his horse to one side of the road, he waited a moment while the drumming swelled, growing louder and louder until it thundered. The pounding made his stomach quiver until finally he saw the source of the sound burst forth from the embankment on the far side. Lieutenant Dobbins had taken his platoon out for a mounted drill. Now he was coming back, bent low over his horse's head, riding at the head of a column of men. The horse's mane and tail were streaming out behind, the steed in full gallop, nostrils flaring wide, powerful muscles and haunches throbbing.

Following Dobbins was the flag bearer, his banner with its crossed blue bars, white stars, and red field snapping in the wind. The rest of the platoon urged their animals onward. When they hit the water, sand and silver bubbles flew up in a sheet of spray sustained by the churning action of the horses' hooves. It was almost like rain.

Even to Rindell the sight of a band of mounted men crossing a stream at full gallop was thrilling. His honor was pledged to a different cause, but he lived, ate, and slept with these men.

He stood on the embankment a moment longer, listening as the thunder receded and died away. Once again the only sounds were the gurgling of the stream, the whisper of the trees, and the songs of birds that were dipping their wings in the clear water and soaring aloft. Slowly, almost reluctantly, he left the pacific stream bed, continuing his journey to Resaca.

A civilian telegrapher was on duty when Mike Rindell arrived at the telegraphy office in Resaca. He showed the operator his military orders, signed by General J. E. Johnston, authorizing him to use the telegraph any time he wished.

"I'll be handling the key myself," he told the operator. "You can stand by, if you wish."

"I'd just as soon go outside for a breath of fresh air, Captain."

The telegrapher knew Rindell, who had used the telegraph before. In fact, Mike Rindell was a skilled telegrapher. He was also a civil engineer and could drive a steam engine. It was the diversity of his talent that had brought Matthew Faraday to recruit him five years before.

The war had not yet started then, and Rindell had found working for Matthew Faraday exciting. But when the war began, he had been eager to get into battle. He went to Matthew Faraday and told him that he wished to resign from the agency so he could join the army.

Faraday had not tried to talk him out of it. Instead, he had asked him to dinner, requesting that he come by at six that evening.

"We're going to have dinner with a good friend of mine," Matthew Faraday had promised his young agent. "After that, Michael, if you still want to resign in order to fight for your country, I won't try and stop you."

Mike Rindell remembered laughing. "Maybe you won't try, but I bet your friend will. Well, I'm telling you right now, Mr. Faraday, it doesn't matter who your friend is. I'm determined to go to war. Your friend can say all he wants. It just won't make any difference."

Mike Rindell smiled as he thought of how wrong he had been. . . .

Matthew Faraday greeted Rindell warmly when he arrived for dinner that evening. The aroma of roasted pork drifted from the kitchen, and from the corner of his eye the young agent could see Faraday's servants setting the table in the dining room.

"Come in, Michael, come in," Faraday said effusively. "We'll have a brandy while we wait for our guest."

"Tell me, am I early, or is your other guest late?"

Faraday had just put his cigar back in his mouth. He took it out again and laughed. "My boy, according to protocol, no matter when my guest arrives, he is on time."

"Just who is your guest, sir?"

"Wait . . . your curiosity will be satisfied," Matthew Faraday said, his sharp blue eyes twinkling with anticipation.

Mike Rindell sat comfortably in the chair Faraday offered. He was nursing a brandy and wondering who the mysterious dinner guest might be. He and Faraday spoke of inconsequential things; not once did the subject of leaving the agency come up. Then, at half an hour past the appointed time, they heard a knock at the door.

"Ah, there he is now," Faraday said, rising.

The door was opened, and a short, powerfully built man stepped into the foyer. He looked around the room, then walked quickly to the door leading into the dining room.

"Who's back there?" he asked, pointing to the kitchen.

"Only my cook and a house servant," Faraday replied. "You may open the door and check if you'd like."

The bodyguard walked through Faraday's dining room and pushed open the door to the kitchen. Rindell had been aware of chatter coming from the two black women in the kitchen, but their conversation ended abruptly when the door opened.

"Mr. Faraday," Rindell whispered. "Who is that man?"

Faraday held up his hand. "Be patient, son. His name is Ward Hill Lamon, but he's not our dinner guest."

"Everything seems in order," Lamon concluded, reentering the dining room. "He'll join you in a few moments."

The strange man departed then, leaving Mike Rindell to look at Faraday with curiosity. In response, Faraday sucked on his cigar and smiled.

A moment later, the door opened, and a tall, thin man with a prominent nose and high cheekbones stepped into the room. "Hello, Faraday," the man said, extending his bony hand.

Rindell gasped as he recognized the guest.

"Hello, Mr. President," Faraday said, taking Abraham Lincoln's hand.

The two men shook, the President holding Faraday's hand in his grip for several seconds. Faraday laughed. "All right, that's enough, you win, Mr. President!"

"It's these long fingers," said Lincoln, his resonant voice filling the room. "I could always get the better of somebody in a squeezing contest. The Lord might have made me ugly," he explained to Rindell, "but He made me strong."

"Michael, I'd like to introduce you to an old friend of mine. When I first met Mr. Lincoln, he was a lawyer for the Illinois Central Railroad."

"I was also the counsel of record for an assortment of ruffians and scalawags. Don't forget that," Lincoln said. "You can't always choose your clients when you're getting started in the business of law!"

The three men had a drink in the parlor and then retired to the dining room. The food was served from silver trays and eaten off the finest china. Rindell found the fare excellent and ate heartily, but he noticed that the President scarcely touched his food. At first the Faraday agent thought it was because Lincoln was so busy telling stories that he did not have the opportunity to eat. Later, he decided it was by design. Lincoln had no intention of eating as much as he was given. The story-telling was merely a ruse to disguise a finicky appetite.

"Now, Mr. Rindell," Lincoln said after dinner was over and they had returned to the parlor. "Matthew tells me you're thinking of leaving his agency and joining the army."

"Yes, Mr. President."

Lincoln leaned back in the chair and folded his hands in his lap. "I can understand that. . . . We need courageous and clever young men in the army. But the special assignments we'll be giving Faraday Security Service are likely to be the most dangerous of all. I would never ask anyone but the most willing and enthusiastic volunteer to stay with such a job."

"Special assignments?" Rindell asked.

"Yes, Mr. Rindell," Lincoln replied. "I've always believed that a government, particularly a government at war, is best served by a special agency whose only function is to gather information from the enemy. I believe they call such information intelligence. I have proposed to Secretary Stanton that we set up such an agency under the government, but he informs me that Congress will never approve such a measure."

"Why not? . . . I would think it would be prudent."

"Prudent, perhaps," Lincoln's deep voice avowed. "But you know how people feel about spies. Take Mr. Nathan Hale, one of our country's genuine heroes . . . 'I regret that I have but one life to give for my country.' Now that was a well-turned phrase. But because he was a spy, even the most ardent patriot assigns him a less than honorable position. Then, of course, there's Benedict Arnold, a villain to most Americans though I'm told he was quite a hero to our English cousins. Secretary Stanton is right. Congress would not authorize the establishment of a governmental agency devoted to spying."

"That's where we come in, Michael," Faraday interjected.

Rindell considered what he was hearing. "I thought Mr. Pinkerton's was the official detective agency for the government."

Lincoln smiled. "In some areas, yes. But I've made special arrangements with Matthew to provide us with an agency to deal only with keeping the railroads open."

"I've already accepted the job," Faraday added. "But I can only do it if I have qualified agents."

Mike Rindell chuckled. Leaning back in his chair, he looked at his employer. "I'll give you this, Mr. Faraday. When you call in a friend to make a point, you don't pussyfoot around!"

"I always say you can kill a bear with a well-placed thirty-caliber rifle ball. But with a fifty-one caliber, there's no question about it."

"Yeah? Well, you didn't just bring in a fifty-one caliber . . . you brought in a cannon!"

"Did it work?" President Lincoln asked with a smile.

"Yes, Mr. President," Rindell said. "I won't be leaving Faraday Security Service. . . ."

Mike Rindell tapped the key to open the line to Richmond. According to his time schedule, the operator at the other end was supposed to be a Faraday agent.

"Richmond ready to receive," the return message clattered.

Like most telegraphers, Rindell could recognize the hand on the key at the other end as easily as he could recognize a human voice. Each sender had his own rhythm of sending the specified dots and dashes, as unique as a signature. Rindell recognized the hand of the agent, but to be safe he sent an identifier code.

"Happy birthday," he tapped.

"My birthday isn't until tomorrow," the key snapped back.

It was the proper response. Rindell was now ready to send his message.

First he sent several legitimate messages, requesting timetables for trains using the Louisville & Nashville Railroad. The timetables had proven to be the best information on the disposition of Union forces in and around Nashville. Then he concluded with the coded message.

Meanwhile, as Rindell was just finishing the message, the regular telegrapher returned from his breath of air. The civilian operator stood behind the counter, puzzled by the strange clacks and clicks coming from the key. Finally, he chuckled.

Rindell, who had not heard him come in, looked around quickly.

"Captain, are you sure you don't want me to send the message for you?"

"No," Rindell said a bit nervously. "Why do you ask?"

"Why, those last letters you sent don't make any sense at all."

Rindell laughed. "It's okay . . . the telegrapher at the other end is my cousin. I was just joking with him." He got up from the chair and reached for his hat. "The key's all yours, friend. And, thanks!"

"Thank you," the telegrapher replied. "Any time you want to come do my work, I'm glad to have you."

Rindell left the telegraphy office, mounted his horse, and started back to Trailback. He had done his job. Now it was up to Richmond to get the message through to Washington.

The operator in Richmond filed the messages received in their proper cubbyholes. Messengers came and went all day, picking up the messages and transmitting them to the proper authorities. Some were acted upon, others discarded. One of the messages was put into a cubbyhole marked Alexandria.

"Is the line to Alexandria open today?" the Richmond operator asked a messenger.

"The man on duty this morning got through," the messenger replied.

"Good. I've got half a dozen things to send. Do me a favor, check with all the clerks and see if there's anything else to send to Alexandria. I'll get in touch with them in about ten minutes."

"I'll check."

It was a routine request from the telegrapher. Even the ten-minute wait seemed reasonable. But what the messengers did not know was that in ten minutes a new telegrapher would go on duty in Alexandria. That operator, like the one in Richmond—and Mike Rindell—was an agent for Matthew Faraday. Hidden among the routine messages would be the encoded message sent by Rindell. In Alexandria, it would be given to a special courier, and the courier would take it across Long Bridge and into Washington. It was done a hundred times a day. Once it reached Washington, the message would go to Matthew Faraday.

Faraday would then have Rindell's message—the one warning him of Colonel Jebediah Tyreen's intention to rob the Gold Train.

Chapter 3

THOUGH THE UNION ARMY OCCUPIED MUCH OF VIRGINIA by April of 1864, it was still officially a state in rebellion, and Alexandria was an enemy city. There were some who advanced the idea that the boundary of the District of Columbia should be extended across the Potomac to annex Alexandria to the city of Washington, but that idea had been resisted, so that for the duration of the war, citizens of the belligerent cities could stare across the river and see each other's flags waving defiantly in the breeze.

Inside the War Department, the top brass had a very good reason for keeping Alexandria allied with the South: It was a window to the Confederacy. Daily traffic between the two communities brought information on the innermost workings of the Confederate planners. Of course, everyone knew the flow of information was uninterrupted in both directions, and some even suggested that the South realized a greater benefit from the exchange. Nevertheless, the arrangement continued.

One of those who crossed Long Bridge every day

was a fifty-five-year-old man named John Norton. Norton lived in Alexandria, though for fifteen years he had worked in Washington as a farrier caring for the horses of the Washington Fire Department.

Early in the war Norton had been approached by Southern sympathizers eager to use his ability to function in both communities to their advantage. But since his sympathies were with the North, he had promptly called upon the secretary of war when he returned to Washington. The secretary had wisely decided that it was advantageous to the Union to keep the farrier on good terms with the South, and he had told Norton to accept the offer. Throughout the war Norton had consequently provided the South with bits and pieces of planted information. He had also been instrumental in securing passes between the lines, thus allowing the families of prisoners of war to visit their loved ones. This unique ability had put him in good stead with his Confederate neighbors.

Norton had also been introduced to Matthew Faraday, who had quickly recruited the farrier to the agency's network of agents and couriers. As a part of the agency, Norton's job was to check daily with Faraday's agent in the Alexandria telegraphy office. Norton never actually knew what the messages he carried across Long Bridge to the Washington office of the Faraday Security Service meant. He did not know the code, nor did he make any attempt to learn it, reasoning that the less he knew, the safer he was. Therefore, when he was given Mike Rindell's message to deliver, he had no idea of its content.

Traffic was brisk across Long Bridge that day. Norton guided his mare through the stream of wagons and carts until he pulled up at the Washington end, where soldiers were stopping traffic at random. Norton was thinking that this procedure was much different from the early days of the war, when everyone coming into the city was searched for bombs or other destructive devices to be used on the capitol. Now, when a search was conducted, it was haphazard at best. The soldiers had grown complacent, since no one crossing the Long Bridge had inflicted the slightest damage on the Union. The Union soldiers at the bridge waved Norton through, saying, "Morning', Mr. Norton. How's the wife today?"

"Better, thanks." Norton reached down and patted his horse on the neck. "How about you . . . get a letter from home recently?"

The soldier smiled and pulled the tip of an envelope from the pocket of his jacket. "Yes, sir, got one just yesterday. My mother says the dogwood's bloomin' back in Missouri."

"They'll bloom here soon," Norton replied. "I figure this is the last cold spell."

"Sure hope you're right. The damp is beginnin' to get to me."

Norton continued on to Fourteenth Street, where he saw a bunch of boys poking sticks at a dead cat that was already flattened by the wheels of a dozen wagons. Then he made his way to Tenth, guiding his mare away from a large Rodman cannon that was being moved to a new position. The largest artillery piece in the Federal arsenal, the Rodman was so heavy that it took nine teams of oxen to pull it, and the cobblestone pavement was literally crushed beneath its wheels.

When Norton was safely around the oxen pulling the cannon, he spurred his mare quickly to the front of the building housing the Faraday Security Service's offices, dismounted, and tying his mare's reins to a lamppost, unobtrusively entered the building.

Matthew Faraday was still engaged in private enterprise, often accepting assignments of a nature totally unrelated to the war. He found any case where his agents were not exposed to danger a welcome respite, and today he was enjoying his work on a report involving stock fraud for the president of Great Lakes Railroad. Getting to the bottom of it required a considerable amount of detective work and puzzle solving. Faraday found himself wishing the war would end, so that he could handle more cases like this . . .

and fewer like the one that had killed Sarah Cunningham.

He had just lit a cigar when he heard a knock on the door. Laying the report aside, he stood just as John Norton entered. Faraday removed the cigar from his mouth, walked around his desk, and extended his hand in greeting.

"John, it's good to see you. Come in and have some coffee. It'll warm your bones—especially with a little bracer in it."

Norton laughed and said, "Thanks, Mr. Faraday. I believe I will." Extending his hand, Norton added, "I've got a message for you."

Faraday took the message and laid it on the corner of his desk. Then he showed Norton to a chair and poured two cups of coffee, adding a splash of brandy to each.

"What are they talking about in Alexandria?" Faraday asked as he raised the cup to his lips. "Do they see the war ending soon?"

Norton smacked his lips appreciatively after sipping the hot brew. "I wish I could say that were so, Mr. Faraday. But the truth is, they all seem bound and determined to keep this war going for another four years."

"Damn. They can't really think they're going to win."

"No, sir. I don't think there's a soul in the South that believes they can still win. But they're counting on folks in the North getting tired of it and negotiating a generous peace."

Faraday leaned back in his chair and shook his head. "They're certainly right about people getting tired of the war. I'm tired of it. But I don't think anyone is willing to give away what it took four years to get."

"That's what I keep telling them," Norton said. "But I reckon they got to hang on to something." He finished his coffee and replaced the cup on the saucer. Rising he said, "Thank you for the coffee, Mr. Faraday. I guess I'd better get down to the barn. I've got some horses to shoe."

"Stay warm," Faraday said as he walked Norton to the door.

Half an hour later Faraday himself left the office and took a trolley to the War Department. Huddled by the stove at the rear of the car, he contemplated the message from Mike Rindell that Norton had brought him. Decoded, it read GOLD TRAIN TO BE STOPPED AT SOUTH TUNNEL.

Again there was a reference to the Gold Train. *But what the devil is the Gold Train?* Faraday wondered. Other than the cryptic words on the paper found in Sarah Cunningham's clothing, he did not know of a train carrying gold. *At the southern end of which tunnel will it be stopped? Blast those bureaucrats!*

Faraday had made his agency available to the War Department, providing them with timely information. But sometimes the bureaucrats got so tangled up in their own deceptions that it made Faraday's work all the more difficult. This was the second reference to a gold train he had encountered, yet he still knew nothing about it except that it had cost the life of one of his best agents. Now he was on his way to see Secretary of War Stanton to find out what he had been missing. If Stanton did not give him the information he needed, Faraday told himself, he would go straight to President Lincoln.

Upon arriving at the War Department, Faraday learned the secretary was down by the Potomac, witnessing a balloon launch. He declined to talk to anyone else, reasoning that only Stanton would have the authority to share information involving something so important as gold. Instead he decided to join the secretary in the day's sport.

Matthew Faraday had no difficulty in finding the launch. Even as he approached the Potomac, he could see across the small expanse of water to Mason's Island, where several dozen soldiers and civilians were gathered around a partially inflated balloon. Faraday took the Mason Island ferry, watching as two portable gas generators pumped gas through long, flexible hoses into a large, silver balloon. At first he did not see Stanton, but he did see Phil Hamilton, Stanton's personal secretary. Hamilton was sitting on a rock, observing the scene with great interest. After Faraday had stepped off the ferry and headed in his direction, the young man rose to greet him.

"Mr. Faraday, how did you know we were making an ascension when we didn't tell anyone?" Hamilton laughed. "What am I saying? You're in the business of collecting such information."

"I thought I was, Phil. That's what I need to talk to the secretary about. I was told he was here."

"He's here," Hamilton replied. "One of the valves on the generator isn't working properly. He went over to supervise its repair."

"I didn't realize Secretary Stanton was an engineer," Faraday said.

"He isn't. But you know the secretary. He believes stern supervision is the solution to everything."

Faraday smiled, then said, "It looks as if he's been proved right. The gas is flowing again."

"Stand clear of the envelope!" someone shouted, and the group buzzed with excitement as the balloon lofted sufficiently to rise above the wicker basket. Fully formed and standing on its own, it was still not buoyant enough to hoist the basket above the ground.

"Get the lines secured before it lifts off!" someone called, and half a dozen soldiers rushed to attach tether lines to the craft.

"I'm surprised to see the secretary showing such interest in this operation," Faraday commented to Hamilton. "I thought a disagreement over the use of balloons was one of the difficulties he had had with General McClellan."

"It was," Phil Hamilton said. "But the secretary is not against them on principle. He's just against Little Mac's insistence that he not make a move unless

Professor Lowe tells him it's the right thing to do. You may remember what a difficult time we had in getting the general to move in the early days."

Hamilton, like many midlevel officials, had taken to using the proprietary word *we* when discussing War Department business. It was an overbearing habit in some, but Faraday did not mind Hamilton's using it because the man did not take his own position that seriously.

"Are *we* to understand that the professor has given his blessing to the project, then?" Faraday asked with some sarcasm.

"*We* don't know," Hamilton replied, catching Faraday's drift and laughing with him. "But the government did buy six balloons. Mr. Stanton hates the idea of having all that money invested in balloons and hydrogen generators and not putting them to good use."

"If the secretary feels badly, think about all those Southern ladies who gave up their silks to make those balloons."

"Ah, yes," Hamilton said, laughing. "I remember the Silkdress Balloon. . . . I believe it only made a few ascensions before it was retired. I don't know where it is now, but I always found the name Silkdress more agreeable than the names we gave the Union balloons. Enterprise, Constitution, Washington, United States . . . patriotic names to be sure. But as far as being romantic, they pale before Silkdress."

"Stand by for the ascension!" a soldier shouted.

All eyes turned toward the balloon, where a young infantry lieutenant had climbed into the wicker basket and was holding tightly to the shrouds. When he nodded his readiness, all the tether lines but one were released. As the remaining line was played out, the balloon began to rise majestically. There was a smattering of applause, and the lieutenant in the basket smiled as the balloon climbed into the clouds. Soon it was so high overhead that it looked like a small ball.

"Matthew, what are you doing here?"

Faraday looked down from the sky and saw that Secretary Stanton was walking toward him. With his high forehead, deep-set eyes, and long chin whiskers, Stanton stood out in the crowd. Once Faraday had told him that if the South wanted to cripple the war effort, the secretary was certainly a prime target for assassination. His appearance was so distinctive that a potential assassin would have had no trouble identifying him. But Stanton had merely laughed it off.

"Mr. Secretary," Faraday said brusquely, "I need to speak to you."

"Sounds serious."

"Serious enough that it's already cost the life of one of my agents. I want some answers."

"All right, all right," Stanton said, quickly pointing to a rocky promontory overlooking Aqueduct Bridge. "Let's take a walk where we can speak privately."

The two men reached the promontory, and Stanton sat on a rocky shelf, while Faraday put one foot up on the ledge. "Mr. Stanton," he began testily. "I want to know everything you can you tell me about a train carrying gold. And I should have been told long before now."

"What do you know about it already?" Stanton asked.

"I don't know anything about it, except that it exists. One of my agents was killed last week. Her last message contained the words *Gold Train* and nothing more. Another of my agents is at risk because of it right now. Whatever it is, sir, the Rebels already know about it, and if my agency is going to be of any help to you, I insist that you tell me what's going on!"

"Calm down, Matthew. You must understand, when you make a gold shipment, you try to keep it as quiet as possible. But I guess the sum of one million dollars is too big a figure to keep secret for long."

Faraday let out a soft whistle. "One million dollars?"

"In gold bullion."

"Where on earth is all that money going?"

"Believe me, Matthew, we need three times that much to do what has to be done. As you know, we have reestablished Union governments in the states of Louisiana, Arkansas, and Tennessee. They are being run by military governors, but they need money to operate. Secretary of the Treasury Salmon Chase has authorized one million dollars to be split among the states. That money is being shipped by special train . . . the Gold Train."

"Well, sir, the Rebels plan to stop that train."

"You're as bad as Pinkerton, Matthew. You see a plot behind every bush. They may have plans to stop it, but they're going to find it a little difficult. For one thing, it will be traveling through Union territory until it reaches Tennessee, and even there it will be going through an area that has been won back by our soldiers. There'll be a detachment of troops guarding the shipment, and we plan to send a pilot engine ahead to make certain the track is clear. I don't think there's much danger."

"I wish I could be as certain as you are, Mr. Secretary."

Stanton stood and brushed off his trousers. "Well, come along, and I'll show you the map. Then you'll know how groundless your worries are."

With the balloon still floating high overhead, Faraday, Stanton, and the personal secretary left Mason's Island and headed for the War Department, which was on the grounds of the White House. As Secretary Stanton's carriage started up the long drive, Faraday caught a glimpse of young Tad Lincoln dressed in the uniform of a lieutenant colonel, happily drilling half a dozen privates. Young Lincoln looked over at the secretary to see if he had noticed the drill, but Stanton was too busy with some paperwork he had brought along.

Later, in the secretary's office, Matthew Faraday was shown a large map with the train route on it. He studied the track, following every mile, locating a place called South Tunnel, about fifteen miles north of

Nashville. He realized that was where the Rebels planned to make their move. He chose not to say anything to Stanton, because a plan was already beginning to formulate in his mind.

A clerk stepped into the office. "Mr. Secretary," he said, "Mrs. Mayhew is here to see you."

Stanton sighed and stroked his whiskers. "Has she been waiting long?"

"About ten minutes, sir. She was here earlier, while you were at the balloon ascension."

"Give me a few minutes. Then I'll see her."

Stanton waited until the clerk had left before he let out a disgusted sigh. "I am caught on the horns of a dilemma, as they say. Julia Chase Mayhew is lovely to look at, but she's not a woman anyone wants to see. She's also not a woman to be put off."

"She's the treasury secretary's niece, isn't she?"

"Yes." Stanton sighed.

"I know his daughter, Kate, a very pretty woman."

"Yes, Matthew, indeed she is. But believe me when I tell you, her cousin Mrs. Mayhew is just as pretty and more clever. She's married to General Andrew Mayhew, acting military governor of Arkansas."

"Perhaps I should go. . . ."

"No, don't go, Matthew. Mrs. Mayhew is much too much for one man to handle."

"Very well." Faraday chuckled. "If you feel it's necessary to call in the reserves, I'll stay."

Stanton pulled a rope on the wall behind his desk. Instantly, the door to his office opened, and the clerk stuck his head in again.

"Send in Mrs. Mayhew," Stanton said.

Julia Chase Mayhew did not enter. Rather, she made an entrance, sweeping in with her petticoats rustling and the bright green of her silk shirt sending out glints of light. Her hair was the color of golden wheat, her eyes a shade of green very like her dress.

Fully aware of her beauty, Julia Mayhew used it quite as devastatingly as a powerful man might use his strength. Extending her hand regally, she swept across the room, waited for Stanton to kiss it, then looked over at Faraday, flashing him a large smile.

"And who is this distinguished gentleman?" she asked.

"Mrs. Mayhew, may I present Matthew Faraday?"

"Faraday? I do believe I have heard that name before. Yes, I have. You're some sort of detective or something, aren't you?"

"Yes, Faraday Security Service," Faraday said.

"Why, Mr. Stanton, don't tell me the War Department has had something stolen . . . that you have to get a detective to find it and bring it back."

Stanton laughed. "It isn't quite like that," he said without going into detail. "And now, Mrs. Mayhew, to what do I owe the privilege of your visit?"

"Mr. Stanton, I understand that a special train is being put together to transport gold to the army in the West."

Stanton's eyes grew wide. "Thunder and tarnation," he exploded. "Is it such common knowledge that people are talking about it in the streets?"

"Now, now, don't get upset, Mr. Stanton," Julia chided. "I didn't hear this information in the street. I heard it from a legitimate source."

"Not very legitimate if they are blabbing it to just anyone," Stanton said. Frustrated and angry, he removed his small, rimless glasses and began polishing them industriously.

"I am not just anyone, Mr. Stanton. After all, I am the wife of one of your generals . . . and the niece of the secretary of the treasury."

"It was Chase, wasn't it? Did Salmon tell you of this?"

"No, Mr. Stanton, he did not tell me," Julia insisted. "Besides, I can't understand your concern. I should certainly think a woman of my position would be qualified to know a few of your precious state secrets. And I should certainly think you would have enough confidence in me to know that I wouldn't spread the information about." She suddenly remembered that Faraday was in the room. "I do hope Mr. Faraday can be trusted with the secret."

Faraday laughed, and Stanton laughed with him finally.

"Madame," Stanton said, "it would be most difficult at this point if he couldn't be trusted."

Julia Mayhew's green eyes sparkled as she laughed in agreement. "Yes, I suppose it would!"

"Now, if I may ask, why are you so interested in this train?"

"Mr. Stanton, I want to travel on that train as a special passenger. I want to join my husband in Arkansas."

Stanton reached into his coat pocket and drew out his pipe as he said, "I'm afraid that won't be possible."

"Why not?"

"There will be no passengers on this train. Its sole function is to transport bullion to various places."

"One of those places, Mr. Secretary, is Little Rock." She laughed melodiously. "Isn't that a funny name for a city? Little Rock?"

Stanton had been filling his pipe from a pouch of tobacco, but he stopped when Julia mentioned Little Rock. After staring hard at her for a moment, he tamped the tobacco in his pipe and said, "Mrs. Mayhew, I am sorry, but you simply can't go along. It's too dangerous."

"Dangerous? Aren't you planning to send an entire company of soldiers to guard the train?"

Stanton sighed. "Since you seem to know everything, yes, I am sending a company of troops. But the very fact that the train requires a guard detail of that magnitude should tell you there is an element of extreme danger in this journey. That much gold makes quite a tempting target for the Rebels."

"Suppose I agree to take the responsibility for my own safety?" Julia proposed. "Would you let me go then?"

"I'm sorry, I—"

"Mr. Secretary," Faraday interrupted. "Might I have a word with you? I think I may be able to clear this up."

"Certainly. Mrs. Mayhew, if you'll excuse us . . . ?"

"Of course," Julia replied, smiling graciously.

Faraday and Stanton walked to a corner of the office, where Matthew spoke in a quiet voice as the other man held the stem of his pipe to his mouth and, with a lit match, puffed it into life. "Mr. Secretary," Faraday said, "Mrs. Mayhew's passage would give us a perfect excuse for putting one of my agents on the Gold Train."

"You mean as a bodyguard? What good is one more bodyguard going to do on a train full of them?"

"Not a bodyguard," Faraday said. "More a traveling companion. The person I have in mind is a woman."

Stanton shook his head and said, "I don't know, Matthew. Even if I said yes, I don't think I'd want it to be a woman."

"A man, sir, would arouse suspicion. A woman acting as a companion and servant to Mrs. Mayhew would be free to roam the train without arousing the slightest curiosity as to her purpose. It's the perfect way to get an agent on board."

"You're assuming we need someone else on board."

"You must think so yourself or you wouldn't balk at letting Mrs. Mayhew go along."

Stanton stroked his beard. "Perhaps you're right," he said. "I'll authorize Mrs. Mayhew's passage."

Faraday put his hand on Stanton's arm. "No one must know that Mrs. Mayhew's traveling companion is one of my agents."

"Not even Mrs. Mayhew?"

"Especially not Mrs. Mayhew," Faraday repeated.

"Surely you don't suspect her of anything?"

"I suspect no one, Mr. Secretary, and I hold no one above suspicion. We do know, however, that she has an easy tongue."

Stanton nodded with a smile. "True enough. . . . All right, let's give it a try."

The two men returned to Julia Mayhew, who had been waiting patiently while they debated the issue of her travel.

"Mrs. Mayhew, Mr. Faraday has acted as your advocate in this matter."

Julia smiled broadly, the dimples in her cheeks deepening. Her eyes sparkled brightly. "Why Mr. Faraday, how wonderful of you to speak on my behalf."

"I intend to exact payment," Faraday said, taking her extended hand.

Julia smiled at him with a feigned expression of shock. "Mr. Faraday, you will make me blush, sir. I'm a married woman. I'm not sure what you're talking about, but it sounds perfectly scandalous."

"No, no, it's nothing like that, I assure you," Faraday said uncomfortably.

The flirtatious tone left Julia's voice, her smile altered, and her tone changed from coquettish to sweet. "Then, sir, if it is in the realm of propriety, I shall be most honored to pay whatever ransom you might demand of me."

"It concerns a young woman," Faraday said. "She works as a cleaning lady in my building, but she is from Arkansas. Now that her state is in Union hands again, she wishes to return home. On her own, she hasn't fare enough for the cars, but if you would agree to take her with you as your traveling companion and personal servant . . ."

"Why, that's a perfectly wonderful idea!" Julia gushed. "It will be a long and tiring journey, and a person of my station certainly needs a servant. You tell her that I shall be most pleased to take her into my employ." Julia raised her eyebrows. "Of course, I'm assuming the passage itself is full payment for her services?"

Faraday chuckled. The Gold Train would be a military train, and as such, neither Julia Mayhew nor her "servant" would be charged a fare. The arrangement was perfect for Mrs. Mayhew. She was getting free passage and a free servant.

"I'm sure that will be satisfactory to her," Faraday replied.

"When will the train depart Washington?" Julia asked Stanton.

"At midnight, Friday," Stanton replied.

Her green silk skirts swooshed as Julia whirled around and clapped her hands. "How exciting it will be to leave the city in the middle of the night on board a train full of gold guarded by a company of soldiers! It has all the makings of a wonderful adventure!"

"I hope it proves to be a very dull one for you," Stanton replied.

For a moment Julia did not understand the meaning, but then she laughed. "Yes, yes, I see what you mean. If it is boring, it is safe." She turned to Faraday. "And thank you again, Mr. Faraday, for your advocacy. Please tell the girl to be at the station ready to travel at least one half hour before we depart. I shall be bringing many of my things, and I shall require her help in boarding."

"I'll see to it that she is there on time," Faraday promised.

Just down the street from the War Department, in the lobby of the Exchange Hotel, a tall, handsome army captain sat in an overstuffed chair, reading a newspaper and pulling at one end of his dark mustache. When he saw the pretty blond woman come through the front door, he got up and, without acknowledging her presence, went up the stairs to his room. Locking the door behind him, he removed his tunic and lay on the bed with his hands folded behind his head.

A few moments later the door that led to the adjoining room was opened, and the same woman he had seen in the lobby stood on the threshhold. "Was my information correct, Mrs. Mayhew?" he said.

"Yes, Captain Ferguson, quite correct. There really is a gold train going west."

"Leaving Washington, Friday at midnight?"

Julia removed her hat and took out the pins that held her hair in place. Cascades of golden tresses fell to her shoulders.

"How did you find out?" she asked, flouncing onto the bed next to the officer. "Mr. Stanton assured me it was a closely guarded secret."

"Oh, but it is," Captain Ferguson said. "However, as commanding officer of the escort company, I had to be told."

"You?" Julia asked, gasping as she partially sat up. "You're the officer in charge of the guard?"

"Yes."

She raised herself up the rest of the way. "Oh, Gerald, that's not a good idea. We shouldn't be together . . . especially now that I'm going to be with my husband."

The captain sat up, put his arms around Julia, and drew her to him. He could feel her heart beating rapidly in her breast. He ran his hand over her hair, soothingly.

"Don't worry," he said. "You'll find that I can be very remote and cold as a statue. No one will suspect that I even know you."

"It's just that it's so . . ."

"So what?"

"So dangerous," Julia said, pushing away his arms and standing up. She walked quickly to the window. The shade was drawn, but she inched it out with her finger.

"Julia, do you think your husband is going to suddenly appear?" Ferguson asked, rising from the bed. "He's a thousand miles from here."

"I know. But there are others . . . officers who know my husband and know me. If any of them should ever see me, should ever suspect—"

"Why do you think I asked you to meet me here?" he asked, walking over to her. "No officers come here.

Besides, we have separate rooms, and we registered at separate times and under false names. Our secret is perfectly safe."

"I wish . . ." She let the statement drop.

"You wish what?"

"I wish we had never met at that play."

"Ah, yes. *Marble Heart*," Ferguson said, smiling. "It was John Wilkes Booth's greatest performance!"

"Yes, well, I curse Mr. John Wilkes Booth for bringing us together."

Ferguson caressed Julia's neck with his fingers. She drew a breath through half-clenched teeth and, turning toward him, leaned her head on his shoulder.

Quietly he asked, "You don't really wish we'd never met, do you?"

"I . . . I don't know," she said. "I only know that I'm frightened that it's gone too far. I'm frightened to think that you'll be going with me . . . that you might even see my husband."

"I promise you, I'll do nothing during the trip to cause you alarm. But I do intend to exact payment."

Julia's blood turned cold. His words were almost identical to Matthew Faraday's, but Ferguson's words had a more potent meaning. She turned toward him and leaned her body against his, her lips upturned.

"And what exactly do you demand of me?" she asked huskily.

Ferguson drew her to him and kissed her deeply. He did not have to say anything; she knew what he wanted.

Chapter 4

As the train Leah Saunders was riding hurtled through the Maryland countryside toward Washington during the afternoon of April seventh, her head was resting on the shoulder of the man next to her. To the casual observer, the scene was rather like a *tableau vivant* performed from *The Beauty and the Beast.* Leah, in her late twenties with long black hair and deep blue eyes, was delicate and beautiful, while her companion, oversized and fearsome looking, was quite homely. Though some of the passengers wondered how such an unlikely pair had come together, the truth was that the man was a stranger to Leah, who had simply taken the seat beside him as the train left Baltimore.

The train went around a curve, and the car jerked slightly, causing Leah's head to slide off the man's shoulder. Her eyes opened with a start.

He laughed. "Here, careful," he said, "or you'll break your neck."

Leah looked at him. "Good heavens! Have I been sleeping on your shoulder?"

"That you have, girlie, that you have."

"Please forgive me. I certainly didn't intend to impose on a perfect stranger."

The man laughed and his eyes sparkled. "That's all right. You can sleep on me anytime."

"I'm so embarrassed," Leah continued. "Look at your lapel! I've made a mess of your jacket and even your vest."

Leah straightened his jacket and adjusted his lapel, her hands moving swiftly over his person. Flattered by her attention, the big man beamed and smiled. He never noticed one of her hands darting quickly and surely inside his jacket to remove an envelope from his vest pocket.

"There!" she said, flashing him a big smile. "You look no worse for the wear." Then she stood up.

"Wait, where are you goin', missy? We don't even know each other."

"No, sir, we do not. And I think it might be better if it stayed that way. I've made enough of a fool of myself as it is."

"You just gonna leave like that?"

"I thought I'd take a walk," Leah said. "Surely the exercise and the air will wake me up."

Leah started down the aisle, then turned to take one more look at the man. When he looked back, she smiled the same embarrassed smile and hurried on. Once outside, she moved across the platform to the next car, and then the next, until she was standing on the platform outside the mail car. She rapped on the door, and it was opened. Inside, mail clerks were working. In addition, three armed men wearing badges were standing there, one a United States marshal, the other two deputies.

"Ah, Miss Saunders, good to see you're safe," the marshal said. "Did you get the list?"

Leah smiled and held up the piece of paper she had.

taken from her seat companion. "Here it is," she said. "It was in his vest pocket."

"Good work," the marshal said, taking the paper from her, examining it, and then smiling broadly. He handed it to one of the others.

"Boys, this is what we've been looking for . . . the name of every single Rebel spy."

One of the deputies whistled softly. "Would you look at some of the names on this list? A police captain in Baltimore, a state legislator, and the mayor of a big town!"

"Do you have any idea how long we've been trying to get this information?" the marshal asked Leah. He tapped the sheet of paper several times. "A lot of government trains are going to get through safely because of this."

"I'm glad you're satisfied," the black-haired woman said. "It is the intention of Faraday Security Service to make our customers happy."

"I have to confess, when I heard they were sending a woman along, I thought it was a crazy idea," the marshal said. "But I guess you did what no man could have done."

"Nope, a man couldn't have gotten on the train and cozied up to ole' Tanner Dye the way you did," one of the deputies added.

Leah blushed and looked away. She was very attractive, and while she used all the skills at her disposal, including her looks and considerable charm, she had never been in a position where she actually had to sleep with one of her subjects. She was quite adroit at advancing to the very edge of compromise, then dancing skillfully away from actual commitment.

With Tanner Dye, who was a well-known Rebel spy, Leah had not gone very far. A simple flirtation had been enough. Yet Leah wondered about that. While Dye had never been arrested, the Justice Department had him under surveillance, hoping to catch his accomplices in their net. When they discovered that he would be putting a new spy network into place, they had consulted Matthew Faraday. Faraday had sent Leah to do the job, warning her that Dye was slick and intelligent.

"I'd better get back," she said to the marshal. "It wouldn't be good for me to be seen in here. You never know who's watching."

She started back through the train, but on the platform between the third and fourth car, Tanner Dye suddenly appeared. He jerked the door open and stepped outside. The platform was small and open to the wind. The noise was much greater here, and the sway of the cars more pronounced.

Leah took a step backward. "Mr. Dye, what are you doing out here?" she asked.

"That's not the question, missy," Dye growled. "The question is, what are you doing out here? Better than that, where is that piece of paper you took off of me?"

Leah's heart was racing. "Piece of paper? What piece of paper? I don't know what you're talking about."

"You don't, huh?" Dye's eyes narrowed, and his face turned into a snarl. "Then answer me this . . . you just called me Mr. Dye. How'd you know my name?"

Leah, realizing her mistake, tried to cover it. "I heard the conductor call your name."

"You're lyin'," Dye said. "I bought the ticket under the name Smith. That's who the conductor thinks I am."

"Well, I must've overheard someone else talking to you. Maybe at the station in Baltimore—"

"That's another lie," Dye said, reaching out and grabbing her by the shoulders. He shook her slightly and snarled, "Now, you got about ten seconds to tell me what I want to hear, or there's going to be one of those terrible accidents people keep reading about in the papers. You know what I'm talking about . . . woman killed in fall from train."

"Please," Leah said, trying to twist away. "You're making a mistake."

"Where's that paper?" Dye bellowed.

Leah examined the cold light in his eyes. He had made up his mind to kill her. He started to push, and instead of resisting him, Leah went slack. Surprised to find no resistance, Dye lost his balance. Leah was waiting for that. Quickly she squatted, then reached out and grabbed hold of the ladder attached to the side of the car.

Dye, his arms flailing at the empty air in front of him, screamed once, but his scream was drowned out by the sound of the engine's whistle. He fell forward, pitching off the platform. Leah, holding on to the ladder, turned her head and closed her eyes. She did not see him hit the ground, but when she opened her eyes a few moments later, he was gone.

It was after dark when Leah returned to Washington and hired a hackney coach to take her to her apartment on New Jersey Street. Tired and dirty, she was determined to ask Faraday for a few weeks off now that her job for the Maryland Railroad Commission was over. She had been disquieted by Dye's fall from the train, and she needed time to blot the image from her mind.

Trudging wearily down the gaslit hallway, Leah unlocked the door to her third floor apartment. As soon as she stepped inside, she saw him, a man sitting in the dark shadows of her room. For an instant she was frightened. Then she noticed there was something familiar about the way the man held his head. When the little fire-tip on the end of his cigar flared, she sighed with relief and asked, "Matthew, what are you doing here?"

Matthew Faraday turned up the gas lamp on the table beside him. A bubble of light swelled and filled the room.

"I got a telegram from the commission people in Baltimore," he said. "They thanked us for a job well done."

"Did they round up the rest of the gang?" Leah asked.

"Yes," Faraday said. "Nasty business, Tanner Dye falling off the train like that. Are you all right?"

Leah sat heavily in a tufted chair. "I'm fine, but I'm going to ask you for some time off, Matthew."

Faraday puffed on his cigar for a moment, then said, "I'd like to accommodate you, Leah. You've worked so hard. But we've got another job, a job that only a woman can do."

"What about Sarah? Isn't she back from Cincinnati?"

Faraday looked at Leah through quiet, sad eyes. "Sarah is dead."

"Dead?" Leah asked, raising her hand to her head. "How did it happen?"

Faraday told the black-haired young woman about Sarah's telegram. Then he told her about Sarah's body being found alongside the tracks. "She was shot in the back, Leah."

"It's my fault," Leah said, resting an elbow on the arm of the chair. "It's my fault she's dead."

"How can you say that?"

"I recommended her, didn't I? I'm the one that sent her to you last year. I trained her. Evidently, I didn't train her well enough."

"Don't be foolish," Faraday replied. The softness had gone from his voice, and he spoke with a hard, chastising edge. "She knew what she was getting into, just as you did. Everyone in this business knows the danger. As for training, you did a good job with her. She was a brilliant agent."

There was a long pause. Then Leah spoke. "The job you have for me now . . . does it have anything to do with what Sarah was working on?"

"In fact, it does. Sarah left us a message before she died."

Leah's blue eyes filled with tears as she said, "I'd be delighted to work on the case."

Faraday told the agent all the information he had so far, explaining about the gold being transferred to the military generals of the occupied states, and about the warning he had received that the train would be stopped at South Tunnel. Then he decided it was time to tell her about Mike Rindell.

"There's someone else on the case, Leah. He's working with an assumed identity—a spy."

"Someone I know?"

"Yes," Faraday replied, looking directly into Leah's deep blue eyes. "As a matter of fact, you know him quite well."

"It's Mike, isn't it?" she said softly.

"Yes. He's been a Confederate captain for the last six months."

"I see."

Faraday puffed at his cigar and asked, "Can you work with him?"

"Of course I can. It's obviously a dangerous assignment. Sarah got killed working on it. If my life is in danger, then I can't think of anyone I'd rather have with me than Mike. He's one of the best."

"True," Faraday said. "But I was afraid your personal relationship might—"

"I'm not a child, Matthew. I won't run and hide over a romance gone sour."

"You know, I never did know what happened to your romance," Faraday said. "Not that it's any of my business, of course, but the two of you are among my favorite people. I rather liked the idea of you being in love."

"To be honest," Leah said, "I never knew myself. There was no big fight, nothing he did to break my heart, nor I to break his. I suppose it just wasn't meant to be. Our jobs carried us to different places, and the romance just cooled." She smiled then. "Whatever it was, it won't get in the way of our working together. In fact, I'm rather looking forward to it. I hope he is."

"He isn't looking forward to it, because he doesn't

know yet. And he won't find out until the two of you actually meet. That is, if you do meet."

"What do you mean, if we meet?"

"Well, if everything goes according to plan, the operation will be very simple. You won't run into Tyreen's Raiders, and you won't run into Mike."

"Has it gone according to plan so far?"

"No."

Leah smiled. "Then what makes you think it will now?" She pointed to a cabinet. "Fix yourself a drink, Matthew. I'm going to take a bath and get out of these clothes. When I come back, you can tell me what this is all about and what my role is supposed to be."

"A *maid*?" Leah said after Faraday had told her the plan. "I'm to be Julia Chase Mayhew's maid?"

"And traveling companion," Faraday added.

Freshly scrubbed and wearing a dressing gown, Leah lay her head back on the chair and laughed. "Wouldn't my mother love that!"

Faraday knew Leah Saunders's background. She was the daughter of a one-time Lieutenant Governor of the State of Indiana, and her mother was the president of the fashionable Vashon Girls' College. Leah was from one of the wealthiest, most respected families in Indiana, pampered by an adoring family and waited upon by loyal servants.

Nothing in Leah's past seemed suited to the rigors of detective work, yet to Faraday's surprise, she had proved to be a courageous and resourceful woman. The idea of being Julia Mayhew's maid was indeed humorous, for Leah's family had more money and a far better social position than Julia's family.

"I'm sorry about the circumstances, Leah. It was all I could think of at the time."

"No, don't apologize," she said. "It's a great disguise."

"I told her you worked in my apartment building as a cleaning girl," Faraday said. "You're from Arkansas by the way, and now that Arkansas is under Union control, you naturally have an uncontrollable urge to go back."

"I see," Leah said. "Well, I reckon I'll have to practice my twang a bit!"

The Baltimore and Ohio Railroad's depot in Washington D.C. was always exciting at midnight, and the city's being at war made it all the more exciting. Eight trains stood on tracks under the great railroad shed, the highly polished cars reflecting the bright gaslights of the station. An almost carnival atmosphere prevailed, with laughter, good-natured joking, and the constant cry of drummers hawking their wares mixing with the music from a military band.

Scores of soldiers milled around the station, some about to depart happily on furlough, others going to new postings. Fresh, young, untried soldiers in their unsoiled uniforms were entering the station building, bright-eyed and eager for a bit of the glory awaiting them.

Leah arrived at eleven-thirty, as she had been instructed, and stood waiting amidst Julia Mayhew's trunks, cases, and grips. She marveled at the self-indulgence of any woman's traveling with so many possessions, and she felt sorry for the soldiers who were asked to off-load the wagon and load the train with the baggage Julia Mayhew was taking to Arkansas.

"You stand right here and see that they don't damage anything or leave anything behind," Julia ordered her.

"Yes, ma'am," Leah replied.

"And I feel I should caution you right now," Julia said sternly. "I have committed everything to memory. If a dress, a pair of gloves, or even a scarf turns up missing, I will know it. Don't think you can get away with stealing anything or leaving anything behind for an accomplice. If I discover something missing, even if you don't have it on your person, I shall hold you accountable nonetheless. As my husband is the governor of Arkansas, he will deal with you harshly!"

"Yes, ma'am," Leah repeated, stunned at the haughty tone of condescension with which she had been addressed.

Turning from her and beginning to walk away, Julia said over her shoulder, "I'll be in the last car. Join me as soon as the luggage is loaded. I'm sure I'll have something more for you to do before the train departs."

"I'll be there as soon as I can," the young woman called in promise.

Leah watched Julia prance down the brick platform to the last car, which the blond woman boarded, her voluminous blue satin skirts trailing behind her. Then, just before the luggage was completely loaded, another wagon was backed up to the baggage car. While half a dozen soldiers stood by, their weapons ready to fire, scrutinizing everyone on the platform, another seven or eight soldiers loaded considerably more onto the train. The boxes were small, but Leah could tell by the way they were being handled that the contents were extremely heavy. It could only be the gold.

A tall, dark-haired captain must have noticed Leah's preoccupation with the loading process, for he slowly walked toward her, pulling at his mustache. Finally he said, "Miss, is there any particular reason you find loading a baggage car so interesting?"

Sighing, Leah said, "No, Captain," then looked around to see if all of Julia's luggage had been loaded. "It's just that Mrs. Mayhew told me to hurry to her room as soon as her luggage was loaded. By then, she said, she would have something else for me to do."

The captain laughed. "Well, that explains your fascination. My name's Captain Ferguson. Gerald Ferguson. I'm in command of the military detachment on board the train."

"I'm pleased to meet you, Captain Ferguson. My

name is Leah Saunders. I'm Mrs. Mayhew's traveling companion and maid."

"Well, Miss Saunders, if there is anything I can do for you during the trip, please feel free to ask. But if you want some advice, you'd better get back to the last car before Mrs. Mayhew comes looking for you."

Leah's delicate features broke into a wide smile, and she answered, "Thank you, Captain."

Soldiers sitting near the windows in the troop car watched as Leah hurried to the parlor car at the back of the train. The car, which had been added on specifically for Mrs. Mayhew, was outfitted in the front with large, overstuffed chairs and a sofa, making that half look like a living room. The back half contained the sleeping quarters.

Julia Mayhew was sitting in a chair, reading a newspaper, when Leah stepped inside. "It's about time," the blond woman said in a tight, irritated voice. "I was just about to come looking for you. Please see to turning my bed down. I'm very tired, and I don't want to sit up all night waiting for my chamber to be ready."

"Yes, ma'am," Leah answered submissively, though she had to fight to keep from smiling. Julia was playing the lady-of-the-manor role to the hilt. She could not even go to bed unless some lowly chambermaid turned down her covers.

Dutifully, Leah stepped into the back of the car, where the bedroom had been equipped with a large double bed, a dresser and mirror, and a chiffonier. There was also a bathtub with a highly polished brass dressing screen around it. Leah turned down the cover on the bed and fluffed the pillows. Then she went back to the parlor.

Assuming an obsequious stance, she said, "Your bed is ready, Mrs. Mayhew."

Julia yawned, put down her newspaper, and stood up. Stretching for a moment, she replied, "Good. You may sleep anywhere out here that you like. Except, of course, for that chair over there by the window. I believe I shall keep that chair for myself, and I'd prefer you didn't use it."

It was all Leah could do to keep from rolling her eyes. "Yes, ma'am," she managed to say.

"Good night then."

Leah watched Julia strut into her sleeping quarters, her gown billowing behind her. Shaking her head, the dark-haired agent eyed the chair near the window that Julia Mayhew had forbidden her to use. A smile lit Leah's face; it was too much to resist.

Looking at Julia's door, Leah watched the thin bar of light beneath it wink out as the lights inside were extinguished. Feeling a sense of illicit exhilaration, she stepped quietly over to the chair Julia had specifically forbidden her to use. She sat down, settling into it. It was not the most comfortable place in the car to spend the night—the sofa would have been much better—but the knowledge that she had exerted her own will over that of Julia Mayhew made any discomfort worth it.

By the time the train pulled out of the station half an hour later, Leah was fighting to stay awake. When the train cleared the yard and received the signal to proceed at road speed, she was fast asleep.

The next day, Julia was truly insufferable. She ordered Leah about as if she were an entire staff. First, Leah had to bring Julia's breakfast, then make the bed and clear away the breakfast dishes. At noon she brought Julia's lunch but had to return it for being improperly prepared.

In the meantime Captain Ferguson found several reasons to visit the car, and each time his advances toward Leah became bolder and more apparent. Leah decided not to discourage him, since it added to her appearance as a flighty young woman to be flattered by the attentions of a troop commander. And, she found him attractive.

But by late afternoon, the captain's attention to Leah must have become too much for her employer to bear, for Julia told her to stop making eyes at the captain.

"I beg your pardon, ma'am?" the younger woman replied.

"You heard me," Julia hissed. "It's absolutely disgusting the way you throw yourself at him!"

Leah suppressed a smirk. "Mrs. Mayhew, I'm not the one making the advances . . . . He is."

"He's an officer in the United States Army, and you're a maid. I can't understand what he could possibly see in you. I mean . . ." Julia let her voice trail off, and she looked away with a sniff.

It was clear to Leah that Julia was jealous, but she did not understand why the woman, the wife of a governor, would be. Unless *she* was seeing the captain . . . ?

"I'll be more discreet," Leah promised.

"Yes," Julia said, regaining her composure. "You do that."

The rest of the day passed without incident. Julia turned in early that night, and a short time later Leah saw Captain Ferguson at the door. She held her finger to her lips, motioning him to be quiet. Then she grabbed a shawl and stepped out of the compartment, meeting him on the platform.

They were nearly twenty-four hours out of Washington now, and the train was sweeping across the farm fields of Ohio. The sky was alive with stars, and the moon, a bright lantern in the midnight sky, was bathing the woods, hills, and fields in shades of silver and black. The train swayed gently, the wheels clacking rhythmically beneath them.

Leah was thinking about Mike Rindell . . . about his method for calculating the speed of a train by counting the joints the wheels passed over in twenty seconds. She counted for the required time and came up with a speed of thirty-five miles per hour.

"Is the Queen asleep?" Ferguson asked her.

"Yes."

He reached for her and then smiled. "Good."

Leah twisted her arms away from his grasp. "Captain, if you are going to be so bold, I will go back inside."

Ferguson lowered his arms. "You haven't been acting like this," he said. "You've been encouraging me."

"I'm afraid I can no longer afford to be encouraging. Mrs. Mayhew has forbidden it."

Leah saw Ferguson smile, and it told her all she needed to know. It was not just a simple attraction Julia felt for the captain. There was indeed something more.

"Very well," Ferguson said. "I certainly don't want to do anything that would get you into trouble."

"Thank you," Leah said.

Ferguson saluted. "If you'll excuse me, Miss Saunders, I'll see to my men."

Leah waited until Captain Ferguson was gone, and then she went forward through the train, looking for the conductor. As she walked through one of the troop cars, a poker game was going on in the rear. The soldiers not involved in it were sprawled on seats, trying to get comfortable. Rifles, bayonets, knapsacks, kepi caps, and even boots were scattered throughout the car, making it difficult for her to walk through. By now, she had passed through the cars so many times that no one seemed to notice her.

Leah found the white-haired conductor in the car behind the engine, walking toward the exit.

"Sir, I need to speak to you," she said. "Right away."

The conductor sighed. "You're the girl working for Mrs. Mayhew, aren't you? What's her highness want now? Is the train riding too rough for her?"

Leah smiled and shook her head. "No, it has nothing to do with her." She pulled a letter from her pocket. "I'm going to ask you to do something rather strange. Please believe me when I tell you there's a good reason for it. When you read this letter, you will see that I have a certain authorization."

"For what? What is it you're going to ask?"

"I want you to change the route of the train."

The white-haired man knit his thick eyebrows and peered at her. "Are you crazy, Miss? This here's a government train, and in case you didn't know, it's carryin' somethin' mighty important. I'm not talkin' about Mrs. Mayhew neither."

"I know we're carrying a million dollars in gold bullion," Leah said. "I also know that our route will take us through South Tunnel."

The conductor was clearly surprised at her knowledge. "South Tunnel . . . uh, that's right. Just north of Nashville."

"We mustn't go through that tunnel, sir," Leah said. "When we reach Bowling Green, I want you to take the Memphis branch. Stay on that track until we reach Graysville, then take the Springfield spur. That will return us to our original course south of the tunnel. Do you know the route I'm talking about?"

"Yes, but that'll add fifty miles to the trip, young lady."

"If it adds a hundred, it's better than going through the tunnel. The Rebels are planning to ambush us there."

His bushy eyebrows shot up. "Now, just how do you know that, miss?"

Leah stared at him squarely. "I can't tell you."

"Well, now, if you can't tell me how you know, why in tarnation should I believe you?"

Leah raised the folded paper and handed it to him. "This letter will help. It's signed by the secretary of war and by the president of your railroad. Please, read it. You'll see that I am acting on behalf of the federal government."

The conductor pulled his eyeglasses from his pocket, put them on, and read the letter. Visibly impressed by the document and the signatures affixed to it, he handed the letter back. Then he asked, "If you're representing the government, what's Captain Ferguson doing?"

"He's the commander of the escort detail," Leah said.

"Don't you think we ought to talk to him . . . see what he has to say?"

"No," Leah said firmly. "We can't do that."

The conductor's eyes narrowed. He scratched his chin.

"Well, now, miss, you got any reason why he ought not to be told?"

"Sir, in my business I've learned that the fewer people who are involved, the better the control is. I'd prefer that you didn't mention the detour."

The conductor looked at her and sighed again. "I'm a fool for lettin' you talk me into this. But if that letter's genuine—"

"Believe me, it is genuine."

"Well, if it is, then I reckon I'd better listen to you. But I do wish you'd let the cap'n in on it. It'd help convince the engineer to do what I ask."

"You're the conductor," Leah said. "I thought you were in charge of the train."

"Well, you're right there."

"Doesn't that mean the engineer has to go where you tell him?"

"Pretty much," the conductor said, flattered by her observation.

"Then we don't need to get Captain Ferguson involved, do we?"

"I reckon not," the conductor said. "All right, I'll tell the engineer. When we reach Bowling Green tomorrow, we'll take the Memphis branch."

Leah let out a sigh. "Thank you," she said sincerely.

"By the way, does Mrs. Mayhew know about this?"

"Oh, no," Leah replied. "She believes I'm on the train to serve her needs." Leah grinned. "And the way she's had me running the past twenty-four hours, I'd say she was exactly right!"

The conductor started toward the front of the train, then turned to look back at Leah. He pointed to the letter. "Miss, I know you got to keep that letter on you, but for God's sake don't lose it. If this all doesn't work out, I'm gonna have to have that letter to show my supervisor."

"Don't worry," Leah said, giving his arm a pat. "You're doing the right thing."

Chapter 5

NORMAN WILLOUGHBY WAS THE CONDUCTOR OF SPECIAL government train number nine-zero-one. Most of the soldiers on board were calling this the Gold Train, and Willoughby had to admit that the name had a certain flair to it. But special government train number nine-zero-one is the way it was listed on his dispatch orders, and he had been a conductor too long to think in any way contrary to dispatch orders.

That was why he was having a very difficult time with the information Leah Saunders had just given him. The young woman wanted him to violate the specific instructions of the dispatch order, and she had a powerfully persuasive tool to back her up. She had a letter, signed by the secretary of war and, more importantly as far as Willoughby was concerned, by the president of his railroad.

Nevertheless, he wished she had not put him in this position. If he changed the route, and the young woman and her letter were a hoax, then he would be in serious trouble. But if she and the letter were genuine and he ignored it, and if the rebels did attack the train at South Tunnel, he would be in even more serious trouble.

He sighed. He could do nothing but order the engineer to change course at Bowling Green, then hope that Leah Saunders was telling the truth. At least he had another twelve hours before the route change would have to be made. He would tell the engineer tomorrow when they were at a water stop.

With that problem temporarily postponed, he continued his walk through the train. As he passed through the first car, a tall, loose-jointed sergeant called out to him.

"Mr. Willoughby, ready for another game of checkers?"

Willoughby pulled his watch from his vest pocket and looked at it, then snapped the case shut and put it away. He smiled at the sergeant. "All right, Sergeant Mills. I reckon we've got time for me to give you another licking. You got the board set up?"

"Sure do," Mills said. "It's up there in the front seat."

Willoughby followed Mills to his seat, and the two men settled down on either side of the board. Mills made the first move, and the game got under way.

"I'm ahead of you two games to one," Willoughby reminded him. "If I win this one, I'll take the best three out of five."

"You ain't won this one yet," Mills replied. He made a move, then smiled triumphantly. "Crown me."

Captain Ferguson came into the car then and stopped for a moment beside the two checker players. "Sergeant Mills, what about our gold shipment? Have you set the guard for the night?" he inquired.

"Yes, sir," the sergeant answered. "Berry and Gilmore have the first relief."

"Still trying to beat the conductor, I see," Ferguson

said, smiling at his sergeant. He sat down across the aisle from the two men and watched the game in silence for a moment.

"You got a jump there," Mills said, pointing out the play to the conductor. When Willoughby took his jump, the sergeant responded by taking three of Willoughby's men.

"Damn!" the conductor swore.

"Cap'n Ferguson," Mills said, stacking the captured checkers in front of him. "There's somethin' been puzzlin' me this whole trip."

"What might that be?"

"Our passengers. I thought we weren't going to have any."

"Yes, well, Mrs. Mayhew is the wife of a general," Ferguson explained. "You've been in the army long enough, Mills. You know that whatever a general wants, he pretty well gets."

"Yes, sir," Mills agreed. "Only it ain't the general's wife that's botherin' me. I'm thinkin' more about the other woman. Cap'n, what do you know about that girl that's supposed to be Mrs. Mayhew's maid?"

"What do you mean, supposed to be?" Ferguson asked, puzzled by his sergeant's strange remark.

"Cap'n, that girl ain't what she seems to be."

"Why do you say that?"

"My ma is a charwoman," Mills said. "My sisters are maids, and I reckon when I get married, I'll be marryin' a servingwoman." He smiled laconically. "That's the way it is in my family. The womenfolk work as charwomen, the men as liverymen. The point is, I know a servingwoman when I see one, and that girl with Mrs. Mayhew ain't one. Cap'n, I think we better keep an eye on her."

Ferguson folded his arms across his chest and looked toward the back of the train, as if he could see through all the cars to where Leah and Julia were riding. "Since you brought it up, Sergeant Mills, I do recall that she seemed to have a more than casual interest in what was going on when we were loading the gold . . . . Maybe I should—"

"Wait a minute, wait a minute," Willoughby interjected. "Captain Ferguson, maybe there's something I ought to talk to you about." Willoughby looked around the car and saw that the three of them were far enough from the others to keep from being overheard. "Sergeant Mills is right. The young lady is not a servant. She's an agent."

"An agent? What's an agent?" Mills asked.

"It's like a spy," Ferguson explained.

"She's a Rebel spy?" Mills asked.

"No, nothing like that," Willoughby said quickly. "I mean, she is like a spy, but she's not spying for the Rebels. She's spying for the Union."

"I don't understand," Sergeant Mills said. He jumped Willoughby's last man, and the game was over. "If she's a Union spy, what's she doin' spyin' on her own people? I thought spies were supposed to go behind enemy lines."

"It doesn't always work like that," Willoughby said.

"Then tell me, Mr. Willoughby, what is her purpose on this train?" Ferguson asked.

"Captain Ferguson, I can't tell you that just yet," Willoughby said. He brushed his hand through his white hair. "Truth is, I've already told you too much. She made me promise I wouldn't say anything about it to anyone. But you two were getting suspicious, so I figured I'd better tell you something, just to set your minds at ease. I'll talk to her tomorrow, and I'll tell her I had to let you two in on who she really was. Maybe then she'll tell you the whole thing. Until then, I'm going ask the two of you not to say anything about all this."

"Why, of course you can count on us," Ferguson said. "Right, Sergeant?"

"Yes, sir," Mills answered.

"I'm only sorry she didn't have enough trust to come to me in the first place," Ferguson went on.

"After all, I do hold my commission by act of Congress. And I am the commander of this guard detail. Any information she may have regarding this shipment should, rightly, be shared with me . . . . As a matter of fact, I think perhaps we should send a telegram back to the War Department, asking for a full explanation."

"No, don't do that," Willoughby said. "I'd rather keep it among ourselves for right now. I promise, I'll talk to her tomorrow."

Suddenly the scowl left Ferguson's face, and he smiled broadly. "All right, Mr. Willoughby. I'm prepared to wait until tomorrow. But I do intend to get to the bottom of this before our trip is complete." He looked at Mills. "And, Sergeant, in my report I intend to see that you get fair mention for your observations. You're a good man to have along."

"Why, thank you, Cap'n," Mills said. He put the last of the checkers in the box and folded up the board. "Mr. Willoughby, we're two games apiece. Finish it tomorrow?"

"Tomorrow," Willoughby promised. He pulled out his watch and looked at it. "Well, I better take another walk through the cars. Good night to you, men."

Mills and Ferguson returned Willoughby's farewell, then watched him until he left the car.

Mills turned to his superior. "Cap'n, you really think we'll find out what's goin' on tomorrow?"

"I promise you, Sergeant Mills, by this time tomorrow, you'll know exactly what's happening on this train. What I'd like to know is why the war department would sneak somebody on board like this . . . . Just what is going on back in Washington?"

One of the things going on back in Washington was a Presidential reception, honoring the organizers of the giant Sanitary Commission Fair that was in progress in New York. The fair was in its fifth day and had already earned more than half a million dollars, every cent of which was to be used to provide hospital care for the war wounded. Matthew Faraday had planned to attend, but he was surprised when he received an invitation to go as the personal guest of Salmon Chase, the secretary of the treasury.

That evening, when he knocked on the door at the Chase home, it was answered by a butler, a white-haired, dignified-looking black man.

"Good evenin', Mr. Faraday," the butler said, stepping away from the door. "The secretary is expecting you. Won't you please come in?"

"Mr. Faraday?" a young woman called as she glided into the hallway to greet him. "Father will be ready in a moment. If you wish, you can join me in the parlor while we wait."

"Thank you, Miss Chase," Faraday answered, moving toward the parlor. Then he caught himself. "Oh, pardon me. I should properly refer to you as Mrs. Sprague now that you are married."

"Please, just call me Kate," the secretary's beautiful, dark-haired daughter replied, smiling brightly. "Paul, would you please bring a brandy for Mr. Faraday?"

"Yes, Miss Kate." The butler turned to attend to the order.

"My, how handsome you look in your formal evening wear," Kate observed, referring to the cutaway jacket and striped trousers Faraday was wearing. "Escorted by such a handsome man, I shall be the envy of every woman at the President's reception. My husband will be prostrate with jealousy."

Faraday cleared his throat in embarrassment. "As I am, actually, accompanying your father, I hardly see myself as a cause for jealousy on the part of your husband."

"Pooh," Kate pouted, her lovely eyes sparkling with humor. "I think a little jealousy would be good for William. All he cares about are his dumb old mills and the availability of cotton." She smiled. "Of course, those dumb old mills have made him an enormously wealthy man," she added.

Kate was wearing a dress of dark blue silk with a full skirt that shimmered and shone as if it had captured its own source of light. For all the fullness of the skirt, however, the bodice looked as if the dressmaker had run short of material, for the neckline was so scandalously low that Faraday was exceptionally aware of her feminine charms. Tall, slender, and exceedingly well formed, Kate Chase Sprague was clearly the most beautiful woman associated with President Lincoln's administration. She had a great sense of humor and an appreciation of life that Faraday enjoyed. This same gusto, however, caused the more proper ladies of Washington society to keep their distance, so Kate had few, if any, close woman friends. Faraday noticed, however, that she did not seem to be bothered by that.

Paul brought the brandy, and Faraday stood by the mantle drinking it, while Kate returned to the chair where she had been sitting. A lantern burned brightly on the table beside her, and a *Harper's Weekly* lay just beneath it. Kate picked up the newspaper.

"Listen to what I just read from 'Humors of the Day,'" she said. "The story is told of a certain New Zealand chief, that a young missionary landed at his island to succeed a sacred teacher, deceased some time before. At an interview with the chief, the young minister asked, 'Did you know my departed brother?' 'Oh yes! Me deacon in his church,' the chief answered. 'Ah, then, you knew him well,' said the minister. 'And was he not a good and tenderhearted man?' 'Oh, yes,' replied the deacon with much enthusiasm. 'He very good and very tender. Me eat a piece of him!'"

Kate laughed heartily at the joke when she finished reading it.

"Really, Kate, I wish you would not allow others to know of your appreciation for jokes of such a callous nature," Secretary Chase said, coming into the room at that moment. "It is unladylike. Help me with this confounded tie, would you? At times like these, I wish the cabinet members could dress in military uniform, the better to be free of such nonsense. Hello, Faraday."

"Mr. Secretary," Faraday said, holding out his brandy in greeting.

"Cabinet officers in uniform? Why on earth would you say such a thing, Father? Let the parlor soldiers strut and fret about, all done up like peacocks," Kate said, as she adjusted the tie at her father's neck. "There are so many of them about now, that they have quite lost their appeal. Those men who will garner the most attention at the President's reception will not be in uniform."

"Kate, is that what you're going to wear, tonight?" Chase asked.

"Don't you like it?"

"It's scandalously low."

"Mrs. Lincoln wears such dresses," Kate replied, tossing her lustrous dark curls. "It's proper to wear dresses in accordance with the style set by the hostess."

"Yes, well . . . Mrs. Lincoln is not young and attractive. You are."

Kate gave a light, lilting laugh. "Father, really, if William isn't concerned by my wearing such dresses, why should you be?"

"Why, indeed?" Chase replied. "Faraday," he said, turning his attention to Matthew Faraday, who had been a bemused spectator to the exchange. "I understand you have dispatched one of your agents to watch over my niece during her trip."

"Yes, sir, I have. She is traveling disguised as a companion and maidservant to Mrs. Mayhew."

Kate laughed. "She must be a dedicated soul to allow herself to act as Julia's maidservant. Julia can be . . . how can I say it without being too harsh toward my kinswoman? Most trying, yes, that's it. Julia can be most trying."

"Nonsense, Kate, Julia is a lovely woman," Secretary Chase defended.

"Of course she is, Father," Kate said, her large dark eyes sparkling in suppressed humor as she smiled at Faraday. "I meant nothing . . . only that she could be . . . *trying*."

"Yes, well, the carriage has been brought around for us. Shall we go?"

Though Matthew Faraday had come to the reception as Secretary Chase's guest, there were so many people who wanted the secretary's time that he found himself alone. For a while he stood to one side of the reception line, watching as men and women moved slowly through, nodding, smiling, and shaking hands with the President and Mrs. Lincoln.

Newspaper accounts made much of Lincoln's being ugly, and his own self-deprecating remarks often referred to it. But Faraday had known Abraham Lincoln for a long time, and he saw the man differently. There was something about Lincoln, whether in the texture of his skin or the depths of his eyes, that softened the President's features. He had a gentleness about him that did not come across in the many photos and woodcuts of the man. He also possessed an ironic sense of humor, and throughout the evening Faraday could hear repeated bursts of laughter from those nearest the President. Yet, for all his joking, there was something sad about him, and Faraday could not quite make it out. It was as though the President knew a great and tragic secret of which he could not unburden himself, and so he had to bear its sadness alone.

As Faraday moved through the room meeting officers, ladies, and high-ranking government officials, he was constantly aware of Lincoln's presense. He almost felt as if the President's eyes followed him, though of course they did not.

Suddenly there was a loud pop, like the report of a pistol, and a woman screamed.

Faraday never traveled anywhere without a pistol, and he had one now, concealed behind his wide cummerbund. Withdrawing the pistol, he moved quickly to the President's side and from the corner of his eye saw that Lamon, the President's bodyguard, had also drawn a weapon. Without saying anything, the two men's eyes met, and each knew that he could count on the support of the other in dealing with this would-be assassin.

Suddenly and inexplicably, there was a loud burst of laughter. Then Faraday saw that Lincoln was leading the laughter, holding up his white glove, the side of which had ripped.

"Don't be alarmed, folks," the President quipped. "I believe when they surveyed this big frame of mine, they came up about an acre short. The popping sound you heard was the seam bursting."

At the President's explanation, everyone laughed, as much in relief as from the humor of the situation. Lamon drifted over to stand beside Faraday. Both men felt conspicuous and a little embarrassed at the guns in their hands. Self-consciously, they put them away.

"I'm glad you were here," Lamon said.

"Why?" Faraday replied, smiling. "To help you in case it had been a real assassin? Or to share the embarrassment with you when we learned what it really was?"

Lamon laughed. "Maybe a little of both," he said.

"I thought as much."

"I had better return to my duties," Lamon said. He nodded toward a short, heavy-set man who was coming toward them. "Here is the chief of police. I shall leave it up to you to explain why we were brandishing our pistols like brigands on the high seas."

Faraday greeted the chief as he approached, but the chief asked nothing about the gun. Instead, after making certain no one was within earshot, he asked if he could speak for a moment about Sarah Cunningham.

"In what regard?" Faraday asked.

"To begin with, have you sent her body back to her family?"

"Yes," Faraday said.

"That's too bad. I would have liked for our medical examiner to look at her again."

"Why?"

"A new piece of evidence has turned up."

"Evidence?"

"Pertaining to her murder," the chief answered.

"I see. Well, speaking for her family, I can tell you that they would not wish to be burdened with the ordeal of a long and painful investigation."

"How do I know you are speaking for her family?"

"I beg your pardon?"

"Mr. Faraday, I know she was not your cousin, as you claim."

"Oh? And what was she?"

"She was your employee," the chief said. "It isn't her family you are worried about. You don't want me to investigate too deeply into what type of work she did for you. Tell me, Mr. Faraday, why was she in the depot yard? What was she looking for there?"

Faraday smiled and looked down. "I thought it was determined that she was killed somewhere else and brought to the track yard."

"Yes, we did believe that at first. But now we have evidence that suggests she was killed right where her body was found."

"What sort of evidence?"

"Before I reply, I would like a few questions answered. What, exactly, was she doing for you?"

"As you know, I am doing work for the war department," Faraday said. "Beyond that, I'd rather not say."

The chief chuckled. "I can't say that I blame you. After all, look what happened in Baltimore. It is supposedly a loyal Union city, just as Washington, and yet the chief of police, the mayor, and many other city officials were found to be corrupted by Southern influence. You don't know whom to trust, and for all you know, I may well be a Confederate spy."

"Yes," Faraday said, neither elaborating nor qualifying his statement.

"Well, I assure you, Mr. Faraday, I am not a spy. So I ask you again. Was she working for you?"

"Again I answer, I would rather not say."

"You would rather not say," the chief said. He sighed in frustration. "It pains me very much to think that the murderer of this young woman is going to go unpunished." When Faraday said nothing, the chief continued. "The evidence I spoke of is a bullet, found on the ground where the young woman's body lay. The same soldier who found her discovered the bullet there the next day. Evidently it had fallen from her body, and that explains why our medical examiner could find a bullet hole, but no bullet."

"Have you got the bullet?" Faraday asked, making no effort to mask his interest.

"As a matter of fact, I do. It's a forty-one caliber bullet. That's not much to go on, I'll admit. But it's more than we had when we started."

"Chief, would you allow me to continue the investigation?"

"You? You mean you want the Washington Police Department to wash its hands of the matter, while you solve the crime yourself?"

"Yes," Faraday said. "You did say that you would like to see the killer brought to justice. I think I can do that. With your help, of course."

The chief stroked his chin. "I don't know, Mr. Faraday. Turning a murder investigation over to private hands, even the hands of a private investigator, is highly unorthodox."

"These are highly unorthodox times," Faraday reminded him. "We are at war . . . and not just with a foreign power, but among ourselves. You said yourself, it isn't possible to know who can be trusted and who cannot. While I do not suspect you personally, the Washington Police Department is composed of many men . . . some of whom may be Southern sympathizers. During the course of this investigation, there is every possibility that some information would come to light that could bring aid and comfort to the enemy."

The chief sighed. "I do appreciate your acknowledgment that I am a loyal supporter of the Union, Mr. Faraday . . . and I will turn the investigation over to you. How can I be of help?"

"I would like the bullet," Faraday said. "And I would like to talk to the soldier who found it."

"Come by my office tomorrow morning," the chief said. "I'll give you the bullet and the name of the man you want to interview."

With the bullet secured in a small cloth bag in his coat pocket, Faraday walked along the track beside the young soldier who had found Sarah Cunningham's body. The yard was quite noisy. Trains were arriving and departing, while in the yard itself small switch engines chugged to and fro, moving cars about to make up new trains.

"She was layin' right here," the young soldier said, pointing to a spot alongside the track. "This is where I found her."

"And the bullet?" Faraday asked.

"It was here, too," the soldier said. "Only I didn't find it till the next day. It was layin' in the rocks, right under where the woman had been."

"Did you find her before or after the *Western Flyer* arrived?"

"Oh, after," the soldier said. "I saw the switchman switch the track and set the signal for the *Western Flyer*."

"And you're certain she wasn't here before the train passed?"

"No, sir, she wasn't."

"How can you be sure?"

The young soldier looked around, as if checking to

make certain no one was listening. "Mister, I'll be honest with you. Me and the other sentry were in drinkin' coffee with the switchman just before the train come by. I should'a been plumb on the other side of the yard. I had to pass right over the place where I found the woman, when I was goin' to the switchman's shack. Then, when I went back to where I was supposed to be, I passed right over that spot again. The first time the woman wasn't there. The second time she was."

"Then she could've been dumped from the train," Faraday suggested.

"If you ask me, there ain't no other way she could'a got there except by bein' dumped from the train," the soldier said.

"Thank you. You've been a big help," Faraday said.

After leaving the yard, Faraday sought out the other sentry who had been on duty that night and talked to him, as well as to the switchman. Neither man had anything specific to add to the young soldier's information, and their stories corroborated his.

The next person on Matthew Faraday's list was the man who had been the conductor that night. Faraday caught him at the depot, standing on the platform under the car shed alongside a train that was about to leave for Philadelphia. It was just a few minutes before departure time, and the conductor, though willing to cooperate, was a harrassed and busy man, and he kept checking his watch, pulling it from his vest pocket and looking at it every few moments.

"I don't mean to be rude, Mr. Faraday," the conductor said, raising his voice to be heard over the sound of vented steam and clanging bells. "But we'll have to be clear of the yard by one-thirty, or we'll be shunted to one side by the arrival of the Boston Express."

"I understand," Faraday said. "Just a few questions, if you don't mind."

"Mr. Conductor, are these the cars for Cleveland?" a man called.

"No, sir, that train is on track three." The man started to run. Again the conductor looked at his watch, then called out to him. "You have ten minutes! You don't have to hurry!"

"Thank you," the man called back, slowing his pace.

"I'm sorry, you were asking?" the conductor said.

"Last week, on the night of the fifth, you were the conductor on the *Western Flyer*, correct?" Faraday said.

"Yes, sir, I was."

"A young woman was killed on board that train, and her body dumped alongside the track."

The conductor's eyes opened wide in genuine surprise. "Look here. Are you telling me that girl they found alongside the track was killed on my train?"

"Yes," Faraday said. "And I would like to know if you have any information about it that might be helpful."

"Why, no," the conductor answered. "What information could I possibly have? I didn't even know it had happened."

"Did you notice anything out of the ordinary that night?"

"What isn't out of the ordinary these days?" the conductor responded. "Soldiers traveling to and fro, young women traveling alone, wounded men going home from the war, recovered men coming back to the war. No, sir, I didn't see anything that night that was different from any other night."

Faraday sighed in disappointment. "Very well," he said. "I thank you for your help."

"Sorry. I don't suppose I was much help to you at all." The conductor pulled his watch from his vest pocket, checked it once more, then stuck it back. "Board!" he shouted. Then he stepped up onto the boarding step of the car, just as the train began to move, the jerking sound transferring down through all the couplers, one by one.

Matthew Faraday had started to walk away when he heard the conductor shout, "Mr. Faraday!"

Faraday turned toward him.

"There is one thing," he called. "A young officer, a second lieutenant, did ask me a rather strange question. I didn't think anything of it at the time, but now, in light of what you were saying, it might be of interest to you."

By now the train was moving at a pace equal to a brisk walk, and Faraday was hurrying alongside it to stay even with the conductor. "What was it?" he called.

"He asked me if anyone had discharged a pistol on the train."

"Why? Did he hear something or see something?"

"He didn't say," the conductor said.

"Do you know the lieutenant's name?" Faraday was beginning to get breathless from keeping up with the increasing pace of the train.

"No, sir. But he was wounded, and he was with Sheridan's Cavalry. I recognized his corps badge."

"What sort of wound?"

"His arm was in a sling!" The conductor had to shout the answer to be heard.

"Thanks!" Faraday called, but his shout was covered by the sound of the train whistle.

As the train raced away, the detective stopped running, watched the train recede, and smiled. This was just the break he was looking for.

Chapter 6

It was a long ride from Resaca, Georgia, to the tunnel where Lieutenant Colonel Jebediah Tyreen planned to set up his ambush, and since the Union had captured Chattanooga in the fall of 1863, most of it would be behind enemy lines. Tyreen left Lieutenant Dobbins and most of his men behind, taking only a platoon. It was, however, a platoon composed of his finest soldiers, men who had proven their courage and resourcefulness many times since the war started.

Rain began to fall shortly after the raiders got started, and it continued for the next several days. The men suffered under the downpour, trying to protect themselves as best they could with their ponchos. Though enduring the wet weather was bad during the day, it was even worse at night, for they could find no dry places in which to sleep. As a result, by the third day the men were as drawn and haggard as ghosts.

Lieutenant Colonel Tyreen was sitting on his horse under a tree, watching his men pass by, and beside him was Mike Rindell, his captain's uniform wet despite his effort to shield it from the rain. The road was a quagmire, and the soldiers were so covered with mud that they were practically indistinguishable from the muck and mire through which their horses were plodding.

"It could be worse," Tyreen observed wryly. "We could be trying to move cannon through this stuff."

"I'd hate that," Rindell said.

"During the battle for Chattanooga, the artillerymen had a saying. They didn't move their pieces on the road, they moved them under the road." The colonel laughed. "I saw more than one gun sink up to its ammunition box."

"It's a wonder you didn't just abandon the guns," Rindell said. "How valuable could they be if they are that unwieldy?"

"Why, my boy, don't you realize that the presence of artillery lends dignity to what would otherwise be an uncouth brawl?" Tyreen asked.

Rindell laughed dutifully.

"There's nothing like a well-placed twelve-pound solid shot for busting up a locomotive," Tyreen continued. "One shot through the boiler, and the train is dead."

"Did you do that much?" Rindell asked.

"Oh, yes. As a matter of fact, on the same railroad we're heading for," Tyreen replied. "We must've knocked over a dozen engines on the Louisville and Nashville Railroad. Not only that, I don't think there's a bridge or trestle we didn't destroy twice over. Even the tunnel we're going to now, South Tunnel, was collapsed a couple of times. I have to give those Yankee engineers credit, though. We would knock them down, and they would build them back up. Rosecrans is a slow and deliberate man, but he is a very effective general."

Mike Rindell was thinking about what Tyreen had said when he saw two riders coming toward them at a brisk trot. In a moment he recognized Ebenezer and Booker, whom he had sent ahead to survey the area.

"Our scouts are coming back," Rindell said.

Major Chambers, seeing the two scouts heading

toward Rindell and Tyreen, left his position in the column and hurried to the tree to hear their report.

"How does it look ahead?" Tyreen asked after the men saluted.

"Lots of Yankees around Murfreesboro and Franklin," Booker replied.

"Can we leave the roads and swing around them?" Tyreen asked.

"Yes, sir. Don't reckon that would be much of a problem." Booker twisted in his saddle and expectorated a large quid of tobacco. It swirled brown in a mud puddle, then was washed away by the downpour. "Truth is, Colonel," Booker went on, "this here rain's maybe a pain in the ass to us, but it's keepin' the Yanks inside their shelters. They don't figure there's any chance of us bein' anywhere aroun', and they ain't all that interested in gettin' out and gettin' wet just to have a look-see."

"Good," Tyreen said. He looked up at the sky. "Let's just pray the rain keeps up until we have at least flanked the enemy."

"Colonel?" Private Ebenezer Scruggs said. "You remember that bridge across Shoal's Creek? The one we took down so many times?"

"Yes, of course. What about it?"

"The Yankees have built it back," Ebenezer said. "They got a big supply depot there in Newton Station."

"Do they now?" Tyreen said. "Well, that's interesting."

"The thing is," Ebenezer went on. "Me and Booker was talkin' about it. We kinda hate to see our good work undone like that."

"What're you getting at?" Chambers asked.

"Well, sir," Booker said. "We'd like to swing over that way and take that bridge down again."

"That's ridiculous," Chambers growled. "Why let 'em know we're anywhere around here? Besides, with everything they've got there, they'd have it back up in days."

"No, wait a minute," Tyreen interrupted. "You know, that might not be a bad idea. We could hit the bridge, then get out. The Yankees would be expecting us to go back to Georgia or Alabama after the attack. That means they would send troops south, to cut us off. What could be better than having them looking for us in the south, while we're robbing the Gold Train in the north?"

"Colonel, maybe they'll send troops after us, and maybe they won't," Chambers said. "They may just figure it's a small raiding party, not important enough to worry about. If we want to be certain to create a diversion, all we need do is start a series of fires in Nashville, maybe burn a few public buildings . . . and the military hospital! Now that's something that would keep them occupied."

"You would burn a hospital?" Tyreen asked.

"Yes, sir, I would," Chambers said easily. "Colonel, those aren't widows and orphans in the military hospital; they're soldiers."

"Wounded soldiers," Tyreen said.

"Wounded soldiers who tried to kill us on the battlefield," Chambers reminded him.

"No," Tyreen said.

"Colonel Tyreen, we are going to hit a heavily guarded train, carrying one million dollars in gold, right in the middle of enemy territory," Chambers reminded him. "We need every edge we can get. Now if we burn their military hospital, the Yankees are going to be running around like chickens with their heads cut off. We can slip right through them."

The colonel turned to Rindell. "What do you think, Mike? Is burning a hospital the only chance we have?"

"Colonel Tyreen, I certainly hope we don't have to stoop that low," Rindell said. The idea was repugnant to him, yet he knew the importance of his protecting his assumed identity.

"Then you agree with me. The best diversion would be to destroy the bridge at Newton Station."

Rindell considered the question. He did not want to

destroy the bridge any more than he wanted to destroy the hospital. He felt obligated to protect all Union railroad property, and the bridge at Newton Station certainly came under that category. Nevertheless, he was adamant about not burning a military hospital. The destruction of a single bridge, perhaps with no loss of life, would be a relatively harmless price to pay to prevent Major Blackwell Chambers from burning a hospital. Besides, Chambers was right when he said the bridge would be rebuilt within a couple of days.

"Yes, sir, Colonel. I'm with you. I think we should destroy the bridge," Rindell finally agreed.

"All right," Tyreen said. "We'll hit it just before midnight, tonight. After that, we head straight for South Tunnel. We'll have plenty of opportunity to be in position by the time the Gold Train gets there."

Tyreen ordered Rindell to turn the column, and the little band of raiders left the Murfreesboro road, then cut across open fields toward Newton Station. They reached the outskirts of the little town at dusk and hid in a heavily wooded thicket to the south, where they made a cold camp. Supper was some stale corn bread and water from their canteen. The smell of coffee and food cooking in the large Yankee encampment just north of Newton Station did not make their cold camp any easier to bear. Tyreen had picked his men well, though, and they were seasoned enough to withstand the hardships. Rindell did not hear one complaint.

Though these men were Confederate soldiers pursuing an objective that was totally contrary to Rindell's mission, he could not help but find much to admire about them. He was not a man given to wishing for the impossible, but he wished there was some way he could reverse the process, so that his mission, and the mission of these magnificent men with him, were the same. War was difficult enough, but when one had respect, admiration, and a genuine fondness for the enemy, it became even more difficult.

"At least it isn't raining anymore," Tyreen said, and Rindell looked up toward the sky, almost surprised to see that Tyreen was right. The rain had stopped, though enough water continued to drip from the trees to make it seem as if it were raining still.

Since the attack on the bridge was not to take place until midnight, Tyreen left two men on alert and ordered the others to get what rest they could. It was cold, wet, and uncomfortable, but Rindell and the other soldiers were tired enough that they dropped off where they lay. Rindell slept so soundly he had to be awakened for the operation.

Tyreen's Raiders circled the Yankee camp and the little town and crossed the fields toward the bridge, moving through the night like ghosts. They had tied down all their equipment that might clink or jangle, and they handled their horses so skillfully that there was scarcely a sound. When they slipped by the encampment of Union soldiers, the loudest sound to be heard was the chorus of rhythmic breathing coming from the tents of the camp.

In the camp itself, half a dozen campfires still smoldered, and little wisps of smoke curled up into the still, night sky. The aroma of coffee and spitted meat was still strong, and the stomachs of some of the raiders growled, though the growls were hard to distinguish from the snores of the sleeping Yankees.

Quickly, and without having to be given specific orders as to what to do, the raiders spread out over the bridge. They drilled holes in the timbers and braces, put torpedos into place, then lit the fuses.

Seconds later, the shock waves of the explosions moved across the field and hit Rindell, making his stomach shake. The fuses had been timed so that the blasts went together, starting as bursts of white-hot flame, then erupting black smoke from the points where the charges were laid. The underpinnings of the trestle were carried away by the torpedos, but the superstructure remained intact for several more seconds, stretching across the creek with no visible means of support, as if defying the laws of gravity. Then, slowly, the tracks began to sag and the ties started snapping, popping with a series of loud reports like pistol shots, until finally, with a resounding crash and a splash of water, the whole bridge collapsed into Shoal's Creek.

"What the hell?" someone yelled from the Union encampment.

"Drummer! Drummer! Sound the long roll!" another shouted, his voice angry and edged with authority.

A single drummer responded to the order, beating the long, open-ended, staccato beat that roused men from their slumber and quickened their heartbeat. Another drummer joined in, then another as the camp turned out to the threat of attack.

"Now, men, this way!" Tyreen called to his little band, and the raiders, bending low over their horses, rode around the west end of the little town. They kept in the tree lines and behind hills until, fifteen minutes later, they were four or five miles away. With most of the Union army in the area headed south to cut them off, they were making their escape north. And it was not actually an escape, for they were not riding to get away from the pursuit as much as they were to keep a rendezvous with a train carrying one million dollars in gold.

Rindell, even as he admired Colonel Tyreen's strategy, breathed a little prayer that his message had been delivered to Faraday, and the train diverted.

On board the Gold Train the next morning, Julia Mayhew was sitting in her special chair, looking out the window at the passing countryside. Leah Saunders was busy with housecleaning chores when Julia spoke to her.

"For heaven's sake, Miss Saunders, would you please sit down? Your constant moving about this car is making me frightfully ill." She patted her forehead with a handkerchief. "Will this accursed voyage never end? The train sickness is most distressing."

"Would you like me to ask the cook for a lemon? Perhaps if you sucked on one . . ."

"No, heavens, no!" Julia said. She sighed. "Why don't you sit down and talk to me. Perhaps if I had something to help me pass the time, other than the constant movement of those horrid trees and ghastly hills outside the car, I would feel better. After all, you are supposed to be a traveling companion, aren't you?"

Leah had become used to Julia Mayhew's insufferably condescending manner, but at this attempt to make her feel insufficient, Leah had to grit her teeth to hold back her anger. "Yes, ma'am."

"Then, please, be a companion for a while."

"Very well," Leah said, settling into a nearby chair.

"Did I tell you about the last party I attended before I left Washington?"

Leah smiled ironically. Julia had not spoken to her at all, other than to issue some demand. "No, ma'am," she answered. "I would love to hear about it, though."

"Well, it was just last week, Friday, I believe it was. The President and Mrs. Lincoln had one of their awful, embarrassing, backwoodsy receptions, and I, of course, was invited to attend."

"Oh, how exciting!" Leah gushed.

"Hardly," Julia responded, raising an eyebrow to show her disdain. "I assure you, Miss Saunders, I am welcome in the finest homes in Washington, so an invitation to a Presidential reception was not something I coveted. However, it would have been terribly impolite for me to refuse, especially as I am the wife of one of the President's most important generals. Therefore, I accepted. It would, of course, have been unthinkable for me to attend unescorted, so I found a handsome young officer who agreed to perform the duty, and we accompanied my uncle, Salmon Chase, who as you may know is the secretary of the treasury. Also present was my cousin, his daughter, Kate."

Julia paused, then said as an aside, "If I recall my social calendar correctly, there was to have been another reception last night. Thank heavens I missed that one. Anyway, when we arrived at the one I did attend, Mr. Lincoln was just inside the door of the room, greeting everyone. A small chamber orchestra played music from the far side of the room, but there was no dancing, as I'm sure you can understand." Julia smiled patronizingly. "No, of course not. How could you understand? Never having been to a party at the White House, you wouldn't realize that the reception room is covered with a thick, rose-colored carpet."

"No, ma'am," Leah said.

"The first person to greet us," Julia went on with her story, "was the President's personal bodyguard, Mr. Lamon. He is at least five inches shorter than the President, but then, so is everyone else. Mr. Lamon gave our names to the President, and I curtsied as I stood in front of him.

"'Mrs. Mayhew,' the President said to me. 'You are the third beautiful young woman to pass before me in as many minutes. First, there was Miss Cameron, then Mrs. Sprague, and now you.' Then the President turned to General McDowell, who was standing nearby, and said, 'General, I have just hit upon a brilliant idea. Suppose we field a division composed only of ladies as lovely as these three? Why, then the enemy would throw down their guns willingly, for who could wage war against such beauty?'

"Well," Julia continued. "You can imagine what consternation I felt over such an uncouth statement. I reminded him in the most resolute voice that my cousin Kate and I were both married to prominent men and were not subject to recruitment into such a brigade as he proposed."

"That must have been most embarrassing to the President," Leah suggested, shifting uncomfortably in her chair.

"Embarrassing? Well, I suppose it would have been to a man of manners. I'm sure, however, that Mr. Lincoln scarcely felt the cut, so insensitive is he to the delicacies of proper society."

The train passed over a small road at that moment, and as Leah glanced through the window, she saw a wagon and mule sitting at the crossing waiting for the train. The driver had abandoned his wagon and was standing at the head of his animal to keep it from being frightened by the train. Just to the right of the road, there was a small sign with an arrow, pointing to Woodburn.

"Woodburn?" Leah gasped aloud.

"What?"

"That sign," Leah said, rising from her chair. "It said Woodburn."

"Well, what if it did?" Julia asked. She had been right in the middle of another recitation, and she found Leah's interruption as irritating as it was confusing.

"That's not possible," Leah said. "I remember studying the map. By taking the Memphis Branch you bypass Woodburn." Leah started for the door.

"Would you come back here, please?" Julia called after her. "I'm sure the engineer knows where to drive the train. After all, it isn't as if we can get lost. This train will only go where the track allows it to go."

"Please, excuse me for a few moments," Leah said, ignoring Julia's call to come back.

Leah left the last car, then started through the soldiers' cars. A few of the men smiled shyly at her, but, as had become the usual custom, most did not appear to notice her. She stopped at the card game that seemed to be in constant progress and asked, "Excuse me, have any of you gentlemen seen Mr. Willoughby, the conductor?"

One of the soldiers looked up at her and shook his head. "Sorry, ma'am," he said. "But I been so busy with this game, I wouldn't have seen my own mother if she'd come through."

"He ain't been through," one of the other players said, shifting the stub of a cigar from one side of his mouth to the other.

As she made her way through the troop cars, Leah got the same answer from eight or nine other soldiers, until finally she was in the forward-most car. Captain Ferguson walked over to her.

"Anything I can help you with, Miss Saunders?" he asked.

Leah looked up at the tall man. "Yes, Captain, I'm looking for the conductor. Have you seen him?"

"He was just through here," Ferguson said. "I think he went toward the rear of the train."

Puzzled, Leah turned to look back toward the rear of the train. "Are you sure?"

"Yes, I'm sure."

Leah shook her head, her blue eyes downcast. "I don't understand," she said. "I was on the last car, and he certainly didn't come in there. And I've passed through every car between that car and this, and none of the soldiers noticed him."

Ferguson chuckled. "Well, that's hardly surprising," he said. "Those who aren't playing cards are either sleeping or so inattentive that they could scarcely be counted on. Come with me. We'll make a thorough search."

Leah was certain that she could not have overlooked the conductor. However, she allowed Captain Ferguson to lead her back through the six cars of the train in a second search. Ferguson had posted guards in the baggage car to watch over the gold, as well as a man at each end of each troop car. The guards stood a duty rotation of two hours on and four hours off for one twenty-four hour period, and then they were replaced by a new squad.

With Leah in tow, Captain Ferguson asked the guard at the head of the first troop car if he had seen the conductor pass through.

"No, sir. I haven't seen him," the guard answered.

"Have you been asleep?"

"Asleep? No, sir. I've been right here, guarding my post, just like I'm supposed to."

"I fear for what will happen if the Rebels decided to try and attack this train," Captain Ferguson said. "You are supposed to be providing security, yet the conductor strolls through this car in full daylight and you claim not to have seen him."

"Captain, he didn't come through this car," the guard insisted. "I have been wide awake the whole time."

"I don't believe you," Ferguson said. "Perhaps the docking of a month's pay will make you more aware of your duties."

"Captain, maybe Mr. Willoughby didn't come through here," Leah suggested quietly. "I hardly think docking this man's pay is—"

Ferguson's eyes flashed angrily as he held up his hand, stopping her in midsentence. "Miss Saunders, I will thank you not to interfere in things that do not concern you. The discipline of my command is a matter for me, and me alone."

"Very well, Captain."

"It so happens, I know the conductor passed through this car, because I saw him. Now, if you will come with me, we shall continue the search."

Despite Ferguson's insistence that he had seen the conductor, no one in any of the cars backed him up on his assertion. When they spoke to Sergeant Mills, he made the comment that Willoughby had been missing all day.

"Why would you say such a thing?" Ferguson asked.

"Why, Cap'n, you know me and him's been playin' checkers this live-long trip," Mills said. "After last night, we're all even-up now. The game this mornin' would decide who got the better of it. He promised we'd play around nine, but I ain't seen him."

Though Leah was certain Mr. Willoughby was not in the last car, she humored Captain Ferguson by going into it with him to have another look. Julia was still in her special chair, staring through the window. When she looked around, she must have seen Ferguson, but not Leah.

"Gerald, I thought I told you not to—" Julia started. Then, seeing Leah, she froze and covered the statement with a hacking cough. Recovering, she went on. "What I meant to say was, how much longer do you think it will be until we reach Nashville?"

Leah heard the amusement in Ferguson's voice as he answered, "About another two hours, I'd say."

"Thank you, Captain." Julia looked at Leah and said, "Well, have you finished your impatient prowling about?"

"No, Mrs. Mayhew," Leah answered subserviently. "I still haven't found the conductor."

"Did he come in here by any chance, ma'am?" Ferguson asked.

"I haven't seen him all morning."

"You're sure?"

Julia fixed Captain Ferguson with an impatient stare. "Why would I say I haven't seen him if I have?" she asked. "He has not been here."

Ferguson sighed, then ran his hand through his dark hair. He smiled sheepishly at Leah. "I'm afraid I owe you and my men an apology," he said. "I was so certain I saw him coming this way. Evidently I was mistaken."

"Then that leaves only the forward section of the train," Leah said.

"We have been forward, all the way to the first car," Ferguson reminded her.

"To the first troop car," Leah replied. "We did not search the kitchen car, the baggage car, or the engine."

Ferguson laughed, then held his arm out in a

sweeping gesture. "If you want to go that far, by all means, be my guest."

"Captain Ferguson, it is very important that I find the conductor," Leah said, leaving the car and starting toward the front. Over her shoulder, she called, "Not only that, I must find him quickly, or it will be too late."

"Too late for what? Miss Saunders, wait!" Ferguson called after her, but she did not stop.

Julia Mayhew was puzzled by what had just been said, but beyond its affect on Gerald Ferguson, she was uninterested. She watched as Ferguson stood where he was for a moment, and then, when she was certain that Leah was gone, she rose and put her hand on his arm.

"Gerald, what is it?" she asked. "What's going on? Why is that girl so insistent that she find the conductor?"

"I don't know," Ferguson said, his eyes still on the door. "But I intend to find out."

"Is it that important?" Julia said. She smiled seductively at Ferguson, and with her hand turned his face toward her. "You've hardly had even a smile for me," she scolded.

Ferguson said stonily, "I thought we were going to keep the proper distance during this trip."

"Well, after I have been reunited with my husband, yes, of course we shall end our relationship. But until such time I would allow a few discreet contacts." Julia stretched her arms up around his neck.

"I think it best for us to stay completely apart," Ferguson said, removing her arms. "Now, if you would excuse me?"

"Gerald!" Julia shouted in anguish as he left the car abruptly. Shocked at his seemingly callous disregard of her, Julia sat back in her special chair and chewed hard on her lower lip to keep from crying.

It's that girl! she finally decided. She was shocked. Certainly Leah Saunders was attractive, in a wholesome, serving-girl way, but why would someone like Gerald Ferguson prefer such a girl to someone like herself?

Julia stared out the window petulantly. She would settle accounts with Miss Leah Saunders. Little Miss Saunders would certainly ask for a letter of recommendation for future employment . . . or perhaps ask her for employment. Julia smiled, as she spoke aloud, composing a paragraph from the letter she would write.

"While Miss Saunders performs the routine duties of housecleaning in an acceptable manner, she must learn that the boundaries of social position are clearly established and should never be crossed."

There, Julia thought, smiling in satisfaction. *That will certainly take care of Miss Leah Saunders.*

While Julia Chase Mayhew composed the letter of recommendation, Leah had already passed through all the cars of the train, including the kitchen and baggage car. She was standing on the front platform of the baggage car, looking at the back of the tender. It seemed unlikely that the conductor would be ahead of the tender in the cab with the engineer and fireman, but that was the only place left to look. If he was not there, he was not on the train. Leah had no idea why the conductor would not be on the train, but if he was not, she had no choice but to try to convince the engineer to stop before they reached South Tunnel.

Passing from car to car on a train was difficult, since a gap of about fifteen inches separated the platforms, which were often of uneven height. But passing from the front of the baggage car to the tender would be more difficult, for there was no platform at all at the rear of the tender. Smoke from the engine curled around behind the tender and burned Leah's eyes. As the car hit an uneven spot in the track bed, it dipped sharply, tossing her forward so that she had to grab onto the side of the car for support. The noise was deafening out here, not only the puffing and hissing of the engine but also the clatter of steel on steel as the wheels rolled over the tracks.

Leah took a deep breath, then leaped forward from the baggage car and grabbed the ladder at the rear of the tender. Her fingers clenched tightly around the rungs, she climbed to the top of the tender, then clambered over the pile of wood that was stacked, ready for use, until she reached the front end. From here she could see the fire burning brightly in the firebox and the quivering gauges of the engine instruments.

Leah understood the instruments, and she knew the workings of the throttle and the brake, for thanks to Matthew Faraday's exhaustive training, she could actually operate a steam engine. She knew what the view was like from the cab, to see the narrow bright line of rails and the slender points of switches as the train rushed forward at thirty, forty, even fifty miles per hour. She had heard the thunder of railroad bridges and seen the track shut in by rocky bluffs as the train swept around sharp curves. She had even been in a cab during dark and rainy nights when the headlight revealed only a few yards of glistening rail as the ghostly telegraph poles lit up, then whipped by so fast as to be a blur.

This train was moving somewhat slower, however, and for that she was glad. It meant that the engineer was a cautious type, one who might listen to her explanation. The fireman and the engineer were at their stations, staring straight ahead, looking for any possible obstructions on the track. Leah realized immediately that the conductor was not with them. That meant that, for some reason, Mr. Willoughby was not even on the train. She feared that some trouble had befallen him, but she did not have time to worry about that right now.

Climbing down to the deck of the engine, Leah reached up and tapped the engineer on the shoulder.

"Here! What the devil are you doing here?" the engineer asked, so startled by her sudden and unexpected appearance that he looked as if he were going to jump out of his skin.

"You've got to stop this train," Leah said.

"What? Stop this train? Are you kidding? Why would I want to do a fool thing like that?"

"Please," Leah said. "If you don't stop it, it's going to be attacked by a group of Rebels."

The engineer laughed. "Rebels? Now, miss, if you had told me that last year, maybe I would've believed you. But we got all the Rebels run out of this country."

"Not all of them," Leah said. "Tyreen's Raiders are going to stop the train at South Tunnel. They're after the gold we're carrying."

The fireman stroked his chin and looked at the engineer. "Charlie, the girl's right about one thing. South Tunnel would be the best place to stop us."

"I don't know," the engineer said. "Seems to me that with all the soldiers we got on here, a man would have to be a fool to try and rob us—especially since the Union controls the railroad all the way down to Nashville."

"Yeah, but what if it's true?" the fireman asked.

"Look, miss, why don't you tell the conductor all this? If he tells me to stop, I will."

"I did tell the conductor," Leah said. "I told him last night. I showed him a letter signed by Secretary Stanton and the president of this railroad. He believed me, and he told me he was going to have you take the branch at Bowling Green. That way we would avoid South Tunnel."

"Well, where is the conductor now? Why isn't he telling us this?" the engineer asked.

"I don't know," Leah said. "I've been all over the train . . . I've looked in every car. I fear something has happened to him."

"Charlie, give him a call," the fireman said. "There can't be nothin' wrong with that."

"All right," Charlie said. He looked at Leah and put his hand on the whistle cord. "I'll call the conductor.

If you really had him convinced, then he'll tell me to stop."

"And if he's not on the train?"

Charlie thought for a minute, then nodded. "All right, if he isn't on the train, I'll back up, all the way to Bowling Green. I'll send a wire from there and get further instructions."

"Good enough," Leah agreed.

The engineer pulled the cord four times, emitting four short whistles, the call for the conductor's attention. The fireman leaned out of the cab and looked back along the side of the train. Normally, the conductor, upon hearing the signal, would lean out from the side of the train and wave.

"See him?" the engineer asked.

"Nope," the fireman answered. "Do it again."

Again there were four short whistles. Again, no response.

The engineer tried it a third time before he looked at Leah, a worried expression on his face. "You say you've searched the whole train for Mr. Willoughby?"

"Yes," Leah answered, relieved that at last someone believed her. "He's not here."

"What are you going to do, Charlie?"

"We're goin' back," Charlie said. He reached for the brake lever and pulled it. The train jerked, clattered, and squeaked to a stop, and Leah leaned against a wall for balance. Finally the train was still on the track, the relief valve venting steam.

The engineer gave the whistle three short blows, signaling that he was about to back up.

"Mr. Engineer, I don't know why you've stopped this train," a voice said. "But I'll thank you to continue on."

Leah, the engineer, and the fireman looked up to the top of the tender and saw Captain Ferguson sitting there, pointing a gun toward them.

"Captain Ferguson, no, it's all right," Leah explained quickly. "I didn't tell you before, but I'm an agent of the Faraday Security Service. We have good reason to believe that the Rebels intend to hold us up at South Tunnel."

"Why should I believe you, Miss Saunders? Mr. Willoughby believed you, and he has disappeared."

"You know that I talked to Mr. Willoughby?" Leah asked.

"Yes, of course I know. I am in command of the military escort of this train, after all. Mr. Willoughby recognized that, and discussed every facet of the operation with me."

"Then you must tell the engineer to stop the train."

"No, Miss Saunders. The only thing I have to do is obey my orders and complete my mission. My mission is to get this train through to Nashville, and that is exactly what I intend to do."

"Miss, I go along with the Captain," the engineer said.

"Captain Ferguson, where is Mr. Willoughby?" Leah asked.

"I don't know," the captain said. "Suppose I ask you that same question? As far as I know, you were the last person to talk to him."

"What are you suggesting?"

"Only that I don't know where he is," Captain Ferguson said. "And I suspect the authorities are going to have some difficult questions for you when we arrive in Nashville."

"But surely you don't suspect me?" Leah stood there, stunned. She had to convince the captain that they were on the same side. "Look, I have a letter from the secretary of war." Leah started to reach for her letter, but Ferguson cocked his pistol, menacingly.

"Miss Saunders, for all I know, you could have killed the conductor. In that case you might be reaching for a gun right now. Well, I don't intend to take any chances. I told you, I have a mission to perform. I am charged with the responsibility of getting this gold through to its destination, and I intend to do just that. If I have to stay right here and keep you under guard until we reach Nashville, then I shall do so."

"Please," Leah said. "Don't you realize you are making a huge mistake?"

"We'll tend to all that when we reach Nashville," Ferguson said. "Now, Mr. Engineer, please proceed as scheduled."

"Yes, sir," the engineer answered. He opened the throttle, and with a jerking of couplers the train started forward again.

South Tunnel was less than fifteen minutes away.

Chapter 7

THE WEATHER HAD TURNED WARM IN WASHINGTON, AND Matthew Faraday raised the window in his office to let in a breeze. Sounds of the city slipped in as well, and he could hear the clatter of hooves and the ring of steel-banded wheels on cobblestone, interspersed occasionally with the laughter of children playing in the street. From a nearby park he could hear the music of a military band, and he remembered having seen a poster earlier in the day advising young and old that the One Hundred and Fourteenth Vermont Band Regiment would be giving a concert.

Faraday was lingering at the open window, enjoying the music, when someone knocked at his office door. When he opened it, he saw a young cavalry lieutenant standing just on the other side, his left arm cradled in a sling.

"Mr. Matthew Faraday?" the young officer asked.

"Yes, and you must be Lieutenant Preston Fletcher," Faraday responded, smiling broadly. "Come in, please. Thank you very much, Lieutenant, for coming to see me."

"You're welcome, sir," the lieutenant replied as the tall, silver-haired man showed him in. "But I must confess that I have no idea why I am here, except that I was ordered to report to your office by my colonel. He said it was an order from the War Department."

"Yes, well, I just wanted your colonel to understand the importance of my seeing you. Please, won't you have a seat?" Matthew Faraday led the lieutenant toward his desk, in front of which stood two comfortable-looking leather chairs.

The young blond-haired man took a seat as Faraday moved behind his desk and sat down. "The colonel also said you are a private detective."

"Yes, I am."

"I've never met a private detective. I'm not even sure I know what a private detective does."

"Well, one thing we do is put together the smallest clues to find people. Like you, for example," Faraday explained with a smile. "I didn't have your name, but I did know that you had been wounded and had recently returned from convalescent leave. I knew you were a second lieutenant, and I knew you were a member of Sheridan's Cavalry Corps." Faraday reached across his desk toward a leather-covered humidor. "I must say, I'm rather proud of the work I did in finding you."

"Found me for what purpose, sir?"

By gesture, Faraday offered Fletcher a cigar, which the young man refused. "Lieutenant, were you a passenger on the *Western Flyer* that arrived in Washington on the night of April fifth?"

"Yes, sir, I was," the lieutenant answered, shifting forward in the chair. "As you said, I was returning from a convalescent leave. But I had full authorization, and I returned on time."

"Lieutenant, please, there is nothing about your conduct that's in question here. I just wanted to know if you were on the *Western Flyer* that night."

"Yes, sir, I was."

"Are you aware, perhaps from the newspapers or

from gossip, that a young woman's body was found by the tracks that same night?"

"No sir, I'm afraid I haven't heard anything about it."

Faraday reached over his desk, picked up a file folder, opened it, and removed a photograph of Sarah Cunningham. "This was the woman. Have you ever seen her? Perhaps on the train?"

Fletcher studied the picture for a long moment, then shook his head. "No, sir, I don't recall having seen her. Did she fall from the train?"

"In a manner of speaking, yes," Faraday said. "Actually, she was shot, then was thrown or fell from the train."

"Shot? You mean murdered?"

Faraday nodded.

"Good heavens, who would want to murder such a young and beautiful woman?"

"This young woman was a private detective, working for me," Faraday explained. "She was working on something for the War Department, and I have every reason to believe she was killed by a Rebel spy."

Lieutenant Fletcher shook his head. "Then that's one spy I wouldn't mind seeing hang at all."

Matthew Faraday leaned forward and, elbows resting on the desk, clasped his hands. "Lieutenant, do you recall asking the conductor if a pistol had been discharged from the train that night?"

Fletcher smiled sheepishly. "Is that what all this is about?" he asked. "Yes, I did ask him, but it was a dumb question, and I felt very foolish afterward."

"Why did you ask it?"

"Mr. Faraday, I'm afraid I was feeling a little nervous about returning to active duty. You see, I was in a dozen or more fights before I got wounded. I thought I was invincible. I would see men all around me getting shot, but no bullets could touch me. Well, one did, and it made me realize that perhaps I have no secret armor after all. The bullet that hit me in the arm could have as easily hit me in the heart or the head. Anyway, now I sometimes think that a thunderclap is a battery of artillery, a glint of light a muzzle flash, the mere closing of a door a pistol shot." He laughed in embarrassment. "I have become what we in the army call a Nervous Nellie."

Faraday smiled with understanding. "Yes, well, anyone who has been exposed to battle is certainly entitled to such alarm. But did you hear something that night? A pistol shot perhaps?"

Lieutenant Fletcher was thoughtful for a moment. "No," he said. "No, it was something else. I smelled it."

"You smelled it?"

"The smell of expended gunpowder," he said. "As I recall, it was just after a man in civilian clothes came into the same car I was in. He had a pistol stuck in his belt, and I thought it smelled as if it had just been fired . . . though, of course, that didn't seem possible."

"It is possible, Lieutenant. Now, if you would, I have a small workroom, a laboratory of sorts, behind my office. I want to show you the bullet that killed Sarah Cunningham. If you can identify the pistol the man was carrying, and if it matches with the bullet the police gave me, it is very likely that the man you are talking about is the murderer."

"I know the type of pistol he was carrying," Fletcher said. "It was a—"

Faraday held up his hand to stop the lieutenant from blurting out the name. "Write it on a piece of paper," he said. "You see, I don't want to be influenced by what you say. I have already examined the bullet and identified the weapon. I'll show it to you, and then we will compare notes. If they match, we may be on the trail of the killer."

Back in northern Tennessee on board the Gold Train, Sergeant Mills had grown tired of waiting for Norman Willoughby to show up for the checker game. So, as Leah had earlier in the morning, Sergeant Mills began moving through the train, looking for his friend. When he could not find him, Mills began questioning the other soldiers as to whether or not they had seen the conductor. None of them had. With no luck in finding the conductor in any of the cars, Mills went forward to the kitchen car, talked to the cooks with no success, then went to the baggage car.

The baggage car was practically empty. Its only contents were the bags and trunk that belonged to Julia Mayhew and the little wooden boxes of gold stacked in the middle of the floor. Two soldiers stood on duty in the baggage car at all times, and one of them was sitting in a chair, tipped back against the front wall of the car, and reading a newspaper. The other guard was at the side of the car with the big sliding door open about one quarter of the way. The soldier was just standing there, looking out of the train, watching the scenery.

The train was passing through particularly pretty country at the moment. Sometimes the track bed was high on the side of a hill, so that a passenger could look far down into fertile valleys full of newly planted fields. Other times the track passed through a valley itself, and the train's occupants could look up onto the sides of the hills at the spring beauty of blooming dogwood and redbud trees.

The soldier who was reading the newspaper looked up when the sergeant came into the car. "What's up, Sergeant Mills?" he said. "Time for our relief already?"

"Not yet," Mills replied. He scratched his head. "Say, have either one of you fellas seen the conductor anywhere?"

"Not me," the seated soldier answered.

"Me neither," the other man replied. "Look out there, Sarge. You ever seen anything as pretty as all them trees and wildflowers?"

"Looks nice," Mills agreed.

The soldier in the door looked around at him. "Somethin' wrong that you need the conductor?"

"No," Mills answered. "It's just that we been playin' checkers, only he didn't show up today."

"Maybe he got tired of your cheatin'," the soldier in the door teased.

"No," Mills said, not taking the bait. "There's more to it than that. I don't believe he's even on the train. A little bit earlier, Captain Ferguson and the lady that's travelin' with Mrs. Mayhew was lookin' for him."

"Well, did they find him?"

"No," Mills said. "And the thing that's troubling me most right now is that now he and Miss Saunders are missin', too."

The man reading the newspaper laughed. "Careful, Sergeant. They may have gone to see their maker. You keep on lookin' for this missin' conductor, you might wind up just like them."

Back in Washington, Lieutenant Preston Fletcher stood bent over a table in the workroom of Matthew Faraday's office. The air was smoky from Faraday's cigar, which the tall, broad-shouldered detective puffed at anxiously as the lieutenant examined the bullet under a magnifying glass. The younger man was quiet for several moments.

"That is what they call a Saxon bullet," Faraday explained. "Notice the markings left by the rifling in the barrel. If you look closely, you will see that the rifling imparted a left-hand twist."

"Yes, I see," Fletcher said.

"There's only one pistol that has a left-hand rifling and will fire a forty-one caliber Saxon bullet," Faraday said.

"And what pistol would that be, Mr. Faraday?"

"I hope it is the pistol you have written on your piece of paper, Lieutenant. I hope it is a Lefaucheaux pin-fire revolver."

The lieutenant stood up, unfolded the paper, and showed Faraday what he had written. It was the Lefaucheaux.

Faraday snapped his fingers. "I was certain of it."

"I saw the murderer, didn't I, Mr. Faraday?"

Faraday was silent for a moment. Then he pulled the cigar from his mouth and studied the tip. "Yes, Lieutenant Fletcher, I believe you did. Now, you were a big help to me with the gun. Do you think you can describe the man you saw well enough for my artist to do a drawing?"

"Yes, sir, I think I can," Fletcher said.

"Come," Faraday said. "I use a young man who has a portrait studio just down the street. We'll get him to make a drawing for us."

The artist Faraday used was one of the more popular portraitists in the city. As a result, his shop was always full of customers, often soldiers who were having drawings done of their sweethearts or of themselves to send to loved ones. However, the artist's arrangement with Faraday was such that the detective could command immediate attention anytime he entered the shop. And, as men and women found it fascinating to see a portrait done from a word description alone, there were few who would complain when Matthew Faraday had work for him to do.

As Lieutenant Fletcher described the man he had seen on the train, the artist filled his pages with lines, shadings, and detail until soon the picture of a handsome, dark-haired young man with a mustache began to emerge.

One of the bystanders, an army sergeant, pointed toward the developing portrait and asked, "Why are you putting him in civilian clothes?"

Matthew Faraday's sharp blue eyes turned toward the sergeant, and before the artist could answer, Faraday asked, "Do you know this man?"

"Not that I can call him by name," the sergeant said. "But I've seen him before. He's an army captain."

"Mr. Faraday, the man did say he was a military officer," Lieutenant Fletcher said quickly.

Faraday studied the drawing for a few moments. He

found something about it hauntingly familiar, though for the time being the reason escaped him. Then he snapped his fingers and said, "Lieutenant, I would like you to come to the War Department with me, if you would."

Preston Fletcher looked surprised. "The War Department, sir?"

"Yes. I want Secretary Stanton to see this drawing."

Less than half an hour later the two men were standing in Stanton's office, Faraday's having pressed the secretary's clerk hard to be moved in ahead of all his other appointments.

"Yes, Matthew. You sent word it was very important," Stanton said as he rose from behind his desk and shook Matthew Faraday's hand. "What is it?"

"Sir, this is Lieutenant Fletcher, and from his description, a portrait artist has constructed this sketch of the man that I believe is responsible for the death of Sarah Cunningham, the agent I told you about." Faraday showed the drawing to Stanton. "Do you recognize this man, sir?"

"No," Stanton said, frowning. "I can't say as I do."

"Please, Mr. Secretary, look more closely. Study it for a moment, but disregard the civilian clothes. Picture him in uniform."

Stanton studied the picture as requested, pulling on his distinctive spadelike beard as he did so.

"Well, I must say that it looks a little like Captain Ferguson."

Faraday smiled. "Yes, sir. That's exactly what I thought. Now, Mr. Secretary, I must know if Captain Gerald Ferguson was out of town lately. Might he recently have been a passenger on the *Western Flyer*?"

"I can check to see if he took a furlough," Stanton said, and he stepped to the door and called in a colonel. After he had told the officer what he wanted to know, the colonel left the room.

"While we're waiting to find out, won't you both have a seat?" He gestured toward two chairs and returned behind his desk. As he sat down, he added, "Now, I'd like you to tell me what this is all about."

"Mr. Secretary," Matthew Faraday began, "if it turns out that Captain Ferguson was on that train, then he is the one who killed Sarah Cunningham. And if he is her killer, that means he is a Rebel spy."

"A Rebel spy?"

"Yes, sir," Matthew Faraday answered. "And right now I'd say he is a spy with his hands on one million dollars in gold bullion."

At that moment the door to the secretary's office opened, and the colonel came into the room, carrying a piece of paper. Standing stiffly before the desk, he said, "Mr. Secretary, according to our files, Captain Ferguson returned from furlough last week."

"Could you tell me where he had been?" Faraday asked.

"Yes, sir," the colonel said, looking at the paper he held in his hand. "He went to Cincinnati."

"Cincinnati," Faraday said. "That means he would have returned on the *Western Flyer*."

"Then there's no doubt about it, is there?" Stanton said.

"To be honest, Mr. Secretary, this is only circumstantial evidence, and I'd hate to go to court with it. But we are at war, and some things must be accelerated. Circumstantial or not, the evidence is now enough to convince me that Captain Ferguson can no longer be trusted."

The secretary of war let out a long sigh and leaned back in his chair. "What do you suggest we do about it?"

"I suggest we send a telegram to the train, to the attention of Leah Saunders," Faraday said. "We need to warn her that there is a traitor aboard."

As Mike Rindell waited at the South Tunnel with the other members of Tyreen's Raiders, the lonesome whistle of the approaching train told him the whole story. His message warning about the ambush either had not gotten through to Matthew Faraday in time, or it had been intercepted and did not get through at all. Rindell shook his head with dismay. Preventing the robbery was now all up to him.

Sitting in his saddle, he studied the faces of the members of Tyreen's Raiders. Colonel Jebediah Tyreen's face showed determination. Sergeant Booker and Private Scruggs, like the other enlisted men, sat their horses quietly, stoically, their expressions reflecting obedience and loyalty to their chief. Tough and seasoned men, they all knew they were miles behind enemy lines, but it did not deter them from their mission. But the look on Major Chambers's face was different, and it puzzled Rindell. He was not sure what it indicated, but there was a strange, almost maniacal look in Chambers's eyes.

The next time the whistle blew, Mike Rindell could tell that the train was much closer. The sound made one of the horses stamp its foot restlessly. It also brought Rindell out of his reflectiveness, and he unsnapped the flap on his holster, preparing for whatever opportunity might present itself. Unless the opportunity was golden, he had reluctantly decided that he would have to go along with the others, even to the point of participating in the robbery.

"Captain Rindell," Tyreen said. "Send someone out to flag down the train."

"What if the engineer doesn't stop?" Rindell asked.

"Oh, he'll stop, all right," Chambers said with an evil chuckle. "That is, he'd better stop. I pulled a rail off the trestle at the other end of the tunnel. If the train hasn't stopped by then, we're going to see us one hell of a wreck."

"Major, if this is a regular train, there may be women and children on board," Rindell said angrily.

Tyreen twisted in his saddle and looked at Chambers. "The captain's right," he said. "Who authorized you to pull a rail?"

"I didn't know I had to ask for authorization," Chambers replied sharply. "I was just doing my job."

"Get that rail back in place," Tyreen ordered.

"It's too late for that," Chambers replied. "Besides, may I remind the colonel that this is war? The South needs that gold."

"We don't need it badly enough to kill innocent people for it," Tyreen said.

"Sometimes innocent people get hurt. Surely you remember the women and children who were killed by Yankee cannon fire in Vicksburg? And they were luckier than the ones who died slowly from starvation." Chambers looked at Rindell. "If you don't want the train to go over the trestle, Captain, I suggest you make sure it stops."

"He's right, Mike," Tyreen said. "Get up the track as far as it takes and stop that train."

Spurring his horse, Mike Rindell galloped down the track several hundred feet and began waving for the train to stop.

"Captain Ferguson," the engineer said. "There's a Reb standin' in the middle of the track, wavin' at us to stop. What do you want me to do?"

"Run him down, Charlie," the fireman urged.

"No, wait," Ferguson said. He scratched his head with the barrel of his pistol. "Maybe we'd better stop. They've been known to pull a railing if the train didn't stop."

"Yeah," Charlie said. "Maybe you're right."

"Don't stop! Back up!" Leah said. "We know the track is good behind us. Back up, and we can outrun them."

Charlie turned to Ferguson. "The girl's got a point, Cap'n," he said. "We could—"

"Stop the train," Ferguson said coldly. To everyone's surprise, he leveled the pistol at the engineer.

Leah gasped and then said, "You're in with them!"

Captain Ferguson's dark eyes were riveted on her as he slowly said, "Yes."

"Where is Mr. Willoughby? Did you kill him?"

"I'm afraid I did," Ferguson said blithely, flashing an evil smile. "So you can see, it won't bother me to kill again. Now, *stop the train.*"

Mike Rindell breathed a sigh of relief when he heard the sounds of vented steam and steel on steel as the train began braking. After it had come to a complete stop in front of him, wisps of steam feathered away from the drive cylinders and turned gold in the sun before drifting away.

A Union officer climbed down from the cab of the engine, and Rindell suddenly saw the opportunity he had been hoping for. By stopping the train this far away from the mouth of the tunnel, he had opened up quite a separation between himself and the other raiders. He jumped down from his horse and hurried toward the officer. With any luck, Rindell intended to get aboard the train, which could then back away before Tyreen and his men joined them.

The Union officer had his pistol drawn, and Rindell realized that since he was wearing a Confederate uniform, the Union officer would be on his guard.

Holding his hands up in the air to show that he was not holding a gun, Rindell said, "Quick! Get back in the train and move it out of here! I'm not really a Confederate officer; I'm an agent for the Union! The Rebels are right behind me. They plan to hold up this train!"

Smiling, the tall, dark-haired Union officer pointed his pistol at Rindell and pulled back the hammer.

"Wait! Didn't you hear me?" Rindell said anxiously. He looked over his shoulder and saw that Major Chambers was nearly upon them. The other raiders were just behind. "There's no time to explain!"

"Oh, you've explained all right," the Union captain said. "You've told me you are a spy, right?"

"Yes!" Rindell looked around again nervously, then saw that it was too late. Chambers had already arrived and was dismounting. "It's too late now," Rindell hissed. "Be ready. We'll have to seize our opportunity when we can."

The tall man wearing the uniform of a Union captain laughed. "Funny you should say that, Captain. You see, I have just seized my opportunity. Blackie, my friend," he called to Major Chambers, "did you realize you have a spy in your midst?"

Mike Rindell gasped. He had stepped right into a trap.

The next moment Rindell felt something poke into his back, and he heard Major Chambers snarl, "Watch your step, traitor. You'd best not make a move."

Unable to do anything, Rindell watched the drama unfold. Looking beyond the Union captain, Rindell saw that some of the soldiers had climbed down from the train and were running forward toward the engine.

"Cap'n Ferguson! What is it?" one of them called.

"Booker!" Chambers ordered. "Get these men surrounded."

Signaling to the men with him, Booker and the other raiders surrounded the train.

Then Captain Ferguson called to his second in command, "Sergeant Mills! Put down your arms! We're surrounded!"

"Cap'n, we can fight 'em off!" Mills insisted.

"You want to fight, Yank?" Booker asked, cocking his pistol.

"No!" Ferguson shouted. "I surrender my command! Put your weapons down, all of you!"

Rindell watched as the one named Mills, under direct orders to surrender and not yet comprehending that his commander had betrayed them, put his weapon down. The others followed suit.

"You Yanks on the train! Come on off there!" Booker shouted to them. "Come out and lay your weapons down, then form up in one of them pretty formations you learned in drill."

One by one the Union soldiers stepped down from the train, laid their weapons in the pile with the others, then moved back away from the track to stand in formation, looking on in curious shock.

"Anybody left on the train?" Colonel Tyreen asked.

"Colonel, there's a woman up here in the cab with the engineer and fireman," Ebenezer Scruggs called down.

"Get them down here," Tyreen said.

Ferguson pointed to the rear car. "You will also find a woman in the special car," he said, and then he smiled. "She's General Mayhew's wife, Secretary Chase's niece."

"A couple of you get her out here to join our little party," Tyreen said.

Mike Rindell saw the train's crew crawl down from the engine, closely followed by a young woman with long black hair. Rindell watched the woman with fascination until at last she was close enough to see her face clearly. And then he got his second shock of the day: It was Leah Saunders. When Leah saw him, their eyes held only for a second, and they gave no indication that they knew each other. But Mike Rindell's mind was racing as he reassessed the situation. "What's a woman doing up in the cab?" Chambers asked.

Ferguson chuckled. "She was supposed to be a chambermaid to Julia Mayhew. Turns out she's a spy. A little like this man, I guess," he added, pointing to Rindell.

"I want to know what the meaning of this is!" Rindell heard a woman's voice demand loudly, angrily, as she was brought to the front of the train. "How dare you stop us and take me off like this! Do you know who I am?"

"Ma'am, why don't you just get over there with the rest of the prisoners and keep quiet?" Booker asked.

"Prisoners?" the golden-haired woman gasped. "I will not be a prisoner. I am Mrs. General Mayhew. I assure you, my husband will deal most harshly with you. Gerald," she said as she neared the officers surrounding Rindell, "tell these men who I am."

Ferguson chuckled. "Oh, they know who you are, Julia. The way you're carrying on, the whole world knows who you are."

"Gerald? Julia? Tell me, my friend, is there something between you and the lady that I don't know?" Chambers asked.

"Why, Blackie, I thought you were a Southern gentleman," Ferguson drawled. "Surely a proper Southern gentleman wouldn't ask such a question."

Major Chambers laughed. "Very well, Gerald, I'll leave the secret between you and the lady. We'll just hope her husband doesn't find out, or he may deal *harshly* with her," he said, mocking Julia's warning.

"You!" Julia said, looking at Ferguson in open-mouthed shock. "You are one of them!"

"Yes, my dear, I am."

"You . . . you bastard, you!" she hissed.

"Tut, tut, my dear, such language from the mouth of a lady."

"Well, I ain't no lady," Sergeant Mills said. He spit a chew of tobacco and wiped the back of his hand across his mouth. "So, Captain Ferguson, when I call you a son of a bitch, I want you to know that I mean it."

"Sergeant Mills, while I will accept such language from a lady, I have no intention of taking it from you."

"Then you better shoot me, you bastard," Mills said. "Cause I intend to call you every name in the book."

"Shoot you, you say? Oh, I intend to do just that, Sergeant." Ferguson raised his pistol and started toward Mills.

"Just a minute, Captain!" Tyreen called sharply. "We may be irregular warriors, but we will conduct ourselves in the fashion of civilized soldiers. We do not shoot our prisoners."

"What about our spies?" Chambers asked, looking at Rindell, who had moved over with the other prisoners and was standing between the train crew and Leah. "It is the fashion of civilized soldiers to shoot spies."

"No," Tyreen said. The colonel looked at Rindell, and Rindell saw that the anger in the commander's eyes was mixed equally with the hurt.

"Colonel, I . . ." Rindell started, but Tyreen waved him off impatiently.

"Believe me, Captain Rindell, if we had time for a proper court-martial, I would act as a prosecutor. And if you were legally convicted, I would gladly afix the rope around your neck. But I will not allow you to be summarily shot anymore than I will allow any prisoner to be shot."

"Then what *are* we going to do with the prisoners?" Chambers asked.

"Move Captain Rindell and the woman agent to the rear car," Tyreen said. "Put the soldiers in there, too. That way we can keep them together and keep an eye on them. And take the uniforms off about six or seven of them and have some of our men dress in them. When we go through Nashville, I want everyone to think the Yankees still have charge of the train."

"What about my lady friend?" Ferguson asked. "What shall we do with her?"

At hearing herself called his lady friend, Julia Mayhew's cheeks flamed red. Whether it was caused by embarrassment or anger was difficult to tell.

"Perhaps we should move her into the baggage car with the gold," Tyreen said. "She's not like the regular prisoners. She's our hostage. It could come in handy to have someone as important as she is along. We might have to use her as a poker chip. And if we don't, we'll trade her back to the Yankees. We can demand almost any ransom we want for her, from the release of some of our prisoners, to the payment of a large sum of money."

"Come along, Julia," Ferguson said, sticking his hand out toward her.

"I'm not going anywhere with you," Julia said defiantly. "I'd rather die right here than let you touch me, you traitor!"

"You can get on the train easily or you can get on hard. It doesn't matter to me," Ferguson said coldly.

"Captain, we'll handle it," Tyreen said sternly. "Sergeant Booker, please give the lady any assistance she may need in boarding the baggage car."

"Yes, sir. Ma'am?"

Fixing Ferguson with one last angry stare, Julia Mayhew pulled her skirts up above her ankles, then walked defiantly toward the baggage car with Sergeant Booker.

Ferguson looked over at Colonel Tyreen and saw in the Rebel commander's face an expression of distaste for him as evident as that exhibited by Julia Mayhew.

"I must say, Blackie," Ferguson said to Chambers, though his eyes remained locked with Tyreen's. "It almost appears as if your colonel doesn't like me."

"There is no rule that says I have to," Tyreen said.

"But I rendered you a great service today," Ferguson said.

"You have turned traitor against your own men."

"As your captain did to yours?" Ferguson said, looking over at Mike Rindell.

Tyreen also looked at Rindell. The same expression of distaste was in his face. "Yes," he said. "As my captain did to my men. I find the two of you equally abhorrent. One of you, I must work with. But the other, I turn my back to." Pointedly, he turned his back to Rindell, and then nodding to Chambers, he continued. "Get them on the last car and let's get out of here."

"Who are you going to get to drive your train, Reb?" Charlie asked. "Cause I sure ain't gonna do it."

"I think you will," Tyreen said. "Sergeant Booker, cock your pistol, please."

"Cockin' that pistol don't mean nothin' to me," Charlie said. "You aren't going to shoot me, cause if you do, you won't have anyone to drive it."

"Mr. Engineer, you misunderstand my intentions," Tyreen said. "I don't intend to shoot you, I intend to shoot your fireman. You might be the only one who can drive, but any strong back can fire. Kill the fireman, Sergeant Booker," he said, calmly.

"No!" the engineer screamed, jumping between Booker and his friend. "You said you don't kill prisoners."

"I will not kill a prisoner who, by his incarceration, no longer represents a threat to the Confederacy," Colonel Tyreen explained. "But your refusal to operate this train represents a direct threat to the safety of my men and the fulfillment of my mission. Believe me, sir, when I tell you that I will not hesitate to kill the fireman."

"No," Charlie said. "Don't shoot him."

"Then you'll run the train for us?"

"Yes," the engineer agreed in a small voice.

"I thought you would. Sergeant Booker, you and those men not dressed in Union uniforms will ride in the baggage car with the gold and the lady. The ones in Union uniforms will ride on the platforms between the cars, in full and conspicuous view."

"Yes, sir," Booker said. "Where are you gonna be, Colonel?"

"Major Chambers, Captain Ferguson, and I will ride in the engine cab. Engineer, I'll be giving you a few directions. I expect you to follow them instantly and without question."

"Yes, sir," the engineer answered meekly.

With everyone loaded back into the train, Tyreen and his two officers took their positions in the engine cab. Tyreen sat on the wooden bench and looked up at the engineer. Chambers stood at the window on one side of the cab, Ferguson at the other.

"All right, Mr. Engineer," the colonel said. "Open the throttle and let's go."

As a force of habit, the engineer blew the whistle two long blasts, signaling that he was about to proceed, and then he opened the throttle. The valves hissed, and the wheels spun a couple of times without purchase. Then, catching hold, the train began moving ahead, taking up the slack with a long chain reaction, the cars bumping against each other.

"Better build up the steam," Chambers said to the fireman, and the fireman began stoking the firebox until it glowed orange. Once again, the train was pounding down the track, heading full-steam for Nashville. Only this time, the man in charge had no intention of stopping there.

It was Tyreen's plan to take the train all the way to Atlanta.

Chapter 8

MAJOR BLACKIE CHAMBERS SAW THAT ALL OF THE PRISONers were put in the special car at the rear of the train. Sergeant Mills and the remaining soldiers of the Union guard detail were locked into the section of the car that had served as Julia Mayhew's bedchamber. Since the windows in this part of the car were designed for ventilation but opened only a quarter of the way, there was no way that any of the men could escape through them. The prisoners were as thoroughly secured as if they had been put into a jail cell.

Technically, Mike Rindell and Leah Saunders were not prisoners of war, so they were kept apart from the soldiers. They were directed to the same car's parlor room, where they were handcuffed to the seats. Chambers cuffed Leah to Julia Mayhew's special chair, while Sergeant Booker fastened Rindell to the seat just beside her. After securing his prisoners, Chambers then posted Booker to guard the front platform of the car and told him to detail a private to stand guard at the rear. Booker chose Ebenezer.

"I want you to take particular care of our friend Captain Rindell," Chambers, smiling without mirth, said to the sergeant before leaving the car. "I wouldn't want anything to happen that would prevent him from attending the little necktie party I have in mind for him."

"You'll forgive me, Major, if I decline the invitation?" Mike Rindell said with evident irony.

"Oh, no, you must come," Chambers said. "In fact, you might say I insist upon it." He laughed at his macabre joke, then left the car.

"Sorry to put you in a spot like this, Booker," Rindell said to the Rebel sergeant, who was walking toward the front of the car.

"Cap'n, you're the one's in the spot. I wish it wasn't so, but it is." Booker closed the door and took his position on the platform in front of it, leaving Mike Rindell and Leah Saunders alone.

The two Faraday agents had not seen each other in months, yet they said nothing for several long moments. Finally Mike Rindell looked at the black-haired Leah and decided to break the silence.

"I wouldn't have wished to see you under these conditions," he told her, "but I'm glad to see you again. I thought you were up in Maryland somewhere." He strained at the cuffs, testing their strength, and found them secure.

"I was," Leah replied. She, too, began twisting in her seat, trying to get free. "But when Matthew asked me to take this job, I agreed."

"Did you know I was on this assignment?" Rindell asked.

Leah's blue eyes flashed at him. "Yes."

Rindell looked at her in surprise. "And still you took it? I would have thought you'd ask him to give it to someone else."

"Why should I do that?"

Rindell, feeling somewhat confused by her answer, looked away from her. "I don't know. I wasn't sure you would ever want to see me again."

Leah gave a wry laugh that nevertheless sounded melodic to Rindell. "I considered that possibility," she admitted.

"Leah, I know this is neither the time nor the place to talk about it," Rindell said, "but you've been on my mind a good deal over the last several months. I've thought about you."

"Have you?"

"Yes."

"And what have you thought?"

Rindell shifted uncomfortably as again Leah's blue eyes fixed on his. "I—I've thought a lot of things. I've thought about what a fool I was for letting you go. I've thought about how things might have been different."

"I've thought about that, too," Leah said. After a pause she continued, "Do you remember that night you asked to meet me in Baltimore? We would have the best dinner in Baltimore, you said. Then we would take a ride through the city in an open carriage, looking up at the stars. Do you remember that?"

"I remember." Rindell remembered all too well. He had not gone to their rendezvous at the appointed time, and he had not seen or in any way communicated with Leah since then. Now, at last, he was having to face his guilt.

"It would have been the first time we had been together, just to be together," Leah observed. "Of course, we had worked together, and we had developed what I thought was a genuine affection for each other. But we had never faced the idea of there being anything else between us . . . until that night. That night, at dinner, and during the ride under the stars, we would cross over the invisible line once and forever. Our lives would never be the same." Leah was silent for a moment, and then she went on. "As I waited for you, I rehearsed the little speech I was going to give. I was all ready to give it, but you never showed up."

Rindell flinched. "Leah, I—"

"Oh, do let me go on. It was a wonderful little speech, Mike. It's a shame I never got to use it. By the way, why didn't you show up that night?"

Rindell sighed and was silent for a long moment. "I've asked myself that same question a thousand times since then. And the only answer I can come up with . . . is that I was afraid."

"You? Mike Rindell, afraid?"

"Yes," he said quietly.

"Mike, I've seen you attack armed men with your bare hands. I've seen you leap from the back of a galloping horse onto a speeding train. And now you tell me that the reason you didn't keep your appointment with me that night was because you were afraid? May I ask just what you were afraid of?"

"I was falling in love with you, Leah," Rindell said. "I had never been in love before. I didn't know if I could accept the responsibility of it."

"So you ran from it?"

"Yes."

"I see."

Rindell sighed. The truth was out, and now he could face himself honestly. "I can't ask you for forgiveness, Leah, because I can't forgive myself. It was an act of base cowardice."

"Mike," Leah said softly, "would you like to hear the little speech I had planned?"

Rindell heard the softness in her voice and knew that he had to listen to whatever she wanted to say, by way of atonement if nothing else. "If you wish. But please believe me, Leah, when I tell you there's no invective you can use that I haven't already used on myself . . . no censure more severe than my own. Whatever you are going to say, I deserve it, and many times more."

Leah smiled. "I was going to say, 'Mike, dear Mike, let us not go so fast. I am frightened by what I feel and by what is happening. Please forgive me for staying only long enough to say these cruel words, and hate me not as I walk away. If what we have is meant to be, fate will bring us together again.' "

Mike Rindell looked at her in surprise, his eyebrows rising. "You mean you were frightened, too?"

"Yes," Leah said. "I was just as afraid as you were."

"No," he said, shaking his head. "Not quite. You, at least, had the courage to show up. I didn't even do that. But I promise you this, Leah Saunders. In any future relationship between us, I'll never show my stripe again."

Leah laughed nervously. "That's encouraging," she said. "Encouraging that you actually believe there may be a future for us. I wish I had your confidence that we are going to get out of here alive." She looked around the interior of the parlor car, then out the window at the fields passing.

"Oh, we will," Rindell said almost offhandedly. He smiled at her. "I wonder if we're close enough to kiss."

Leah threw her head back and laughed again. "You want a kiss now?"

"Yes."

Leah leaned her head toward Rindell, and their lips came together tenderly. Then, with their faces just a breath apart, he asked, "Are you wearing your special comb?"

Leah smiled broadly. "And I thought you really did want to kiss me."

"I did," Rindell admitted. "But I knew that if we could get close enough to kiss, we could get close enough for me to get the comb from your hair. Turn your head."

Leah did as he had instructed, and Rindell, using his teeth, managed to pull the carved-ivory comb from Leah's black hair.

"Careful," she said. "Don't drop it."

Slowly and deliberately, Rindell lowered his head, the comb in his mouth, until it was just over his cuffed hands. Then he turned his palms up—as well as he could, under the circumstances—and dropped the comb, catching it deftly.

"Got it," he said with a sigh of relief.

Working in the confined space the cuffs would allow him, Rindell opened the false top of the comb and took out a long, thin skeleton key. Even with the key in his hands, it was difficult to work, because the amount of movement the cuffs left him was minuscule. Still, he managed to insert the end of the key into the cuff's locking mechanism and wiggle it back and forth. A moment later he was rewarded with a *click* as the cuffs popped open.

"You did it!" Leah said excitedly.

"Shhh!" Rindell said, raising his finger to his lips. Quickly he released her cuffs. Then, as she rubbed her wrists, he pointed to the front of the car and whispered, "Go to the door and call Sergeant Booker."

Leah walked up to the door. Standing there, she smiled prettily and called sweetly to Booker, "Sergeant, would you come in here, please?"

"Glory be, miss!" Booker asked, stepping quickly through the door. "How'd you get loose?" He suddenly noticed that Rindell was also gone. "Where's—" he started, but that was as far as he got, because when he turned toward Leah, Rindell knocked him out with a quick punch to the chin.

Ebenezer was taken care of in the same way, and while Rindell cuffed both soldiers to the chairs, Leah opened the door to release Sergeant Mills and the Union soldiers from their temporary cell.

"I'm going to need your help, Sergeant," Rindell said to Mills.

"Who are you, mister?" Mills asked. "And how come you're wearin' that Reb uniform?"

"It's all right, Sergeant Mills," Leah explained. "He isn't really a Rebel. He's one of Mr. Faraday's railroad agents, working for the U.S. government."

Rindell held out Booker's rifle to Mills and said, "Take this. One of you other men take Ebenezer's rifle."

Mills took the rifle and looked at the two Rebel captives, both of whom were conscious now. "What are you going to do?" he asked Rindell.

"I'm going to get the gold back."

"How you plan on doing that? We've only got two guns."

"The first thing I'm going to do is cut this car loose from the rest of the train."

Ebenezer Scruggs let out a guffaw. "You won't get the gold back if the train's in Nashville and you're left out here in the fields."

"Oh, we'll be going to Nashville, Private, but we won't be the ones held prisoner when we do. You and Booker will."

"Pardon, me, sir, but how will we get to Nashville in time to get the gold back if we're on foot?" Mills asked.

"We won't, Sergeant. But word of the Gold Train's being stolen will, if what I have in mind works out. You see those poles out there? They hold up telegraph wires, and I plan to use them to alert the station."

"How will you do that?" Mills asked.

"With this." Rindell pulled a small telegrapher's key from his pocket. "It's called a pocket key, and while I wouldn't want to send any long newspaper articles using it, it's certainly sufficient for our immediate needs. But first we have to get this car loose."

Again Scruggs laughed. "You'll probably lose a damned hand," he said. "And far as I'm concerned, I hope you do, you treasonous bastard."

"Private Scruggs, if it means anything to you, I'm not a traitor," Rindell explained. "I'm a loyal Union man, and I always have been."

"You're a spy, ain't you? That makes you a traitor."

"A feller can be a spy without bein' a traitor," Sergeant Booker said to his comrade.

Mike Rindell smiled warmly at the Confederate sergeant. "Thanks, Booker."

"Don't thank me, Cap'n," Booker said. "I'd as soon hang you for a spy as for a traitor."

"We all fight in our own way," Rindell said. He took off his jacket and rolled up his sleeves, then looked around at Mills. "Sergeant Mills, I'm going to need some help."

"Yes, sir, I'll do whatever I can," Mills offered.

Rindell indicated that Mills should accompany him to the front platform. As they opened the door to the car, the noise from the wheels moving over the tracks thundered in. Once they were on the platform, Rindell pointed down to the connector pin.

"The only way I can get that pin loose is to get down there to it," he shouted to Mills. "That means you're going to have to hold my legs while I dangle over the track."

"You mean you're willin' to trust your life to me?" the sergeant called back. "You don't even know me. How do you know I won't drop you?"

Rindell smiled at Mills. "When Ferguson ordered you to surrender, you were still ready to fight. That makes you all right in my book."

Mills returned the smile. "I ain't gonna drop you, Cap'n. If you go down, I'll be comin' right down behind you."

Mike Rindell chuckled. "Well, thanks, Sarge. The thought of you falling down on top of me is downright comforting." He leaned over the platform rail and looked down at the track. The crossties were whipping by so fast as to be a blur. He took a deep breath and then said, "All right, here I go!"

With Mills holding him by the legs, Rindell stretched out over the edge of the railing, then slid down toward the overlapping sockets, a large pin holding them together. Soon he was hanging upside down, his head moving at forty miles an hour just inches above the track. From here, the sound of the wheels and the blast of wind was a deafening roar. The slightest mishap could kill him.

Slowly, he reached toward the coupler, but the train suddenly passed over an uneven section of track, and the cars twisted and jerked. The unexpected wrenching caught Mills by surprise, and he partially lost his grip. Rindell felt himself slip down nearer to the track, and he almost put his hands down to break his fall. At the last instant he felt Mills's arms clamp around his legs so tightly that it cut off the blood circulation. No matter . . . he would rather have tingling legs than a bashed head.

"Sorry, sir!" Mills shouted down to him. "Are you all right?"

"Yes! Have you got me now?"

"I got you!" Mills answered back.

Regaining his breath and his composure, Rindell reached toward the coupler again. He put his hand on the coupler sockets, but then the cars twisted against each other a second time, and a gap opened wide enough between the sockets for Rindell to stick his hand between the one on top and the one on bottom. An instant later though, they slapped together again. If Rindell's hand had slipped into the gap, it would have been smashed like a pecan in a nutcracker.

Slowly, he stretched his hand toward the sockets again. This time he managed to reach the coupling pin. He jerked up on it a couple of times, but the pressure of the cars held it secure. Time and again he tried to work the pin up, but he could not make it budge. Then, in the normal give and take of the cars, came an instant when the coupler pin could be moved, and Rindell jerked it free.

"Pull me up!" he yelled, and he felt himself being dragged back up. By the time he was on his feet again, a gap of several feet had opened up between the rest of the train and their car.

Mills pointed to a little wheel on top of the car and said, "We can stop ourselves. That wheel sets the brakes."

"No need," Rindell said. "We're going to have a long walk ahead of us anyway. We might as well let the car coast as far as it will go."

Leah came out onto the platform, and the three of them watched the train pull away.

"Hope no one happens to look back," Rindell said.

"They ain't interested in us," Mills suggested. "They got the gold."

"Yeah," Rindell said. "For now."

Sergeant Mills's observation proved to be true, for no one on the main body of the train bothered to look back. The car coasted for almost a mile before it finally came to a complete stop. When it did, Rindell set the brake to keep it from rolling backward, and then he called to the others, "All right, everybody, out of the car."

"What about the two Rebs?" one of the soldiers asked.

"Get them out," Rindell said. "They're going with us."

Rindell climbed down to the track bed and watched as the remaining soldiers came down, one by one. The two prisoners, cuffed together by one hand, climbed awkwardly down with the others.

Seeing that they were well under control, Rindell climbed the nearest pole and tapped out his message. He waited for a reply before making his way down.

"What's next?" one of the soldiers asked Rindell when he was back on the ground.

Rindell smiled. "We're walking to Nashville."

"Wish I had my old mare," one of the soldiers said.

"You got shanks' mare, what else you want?"

Everyone laughed, and the soldiers' spirits seemed to rise somewhat as they fell into a long column of twos, then began marching between the rails, heading for Nashville. It made for a rather ludicrous sight, for six of the men were dressed in their long underwear.

"Don't hardly seem right," one of them muttered. "Hope my wife don't find out about me paradin' in front of a lady in nothin' but my long johns. Miss, don't you be a'lookin' at us now."

"I promise I won't." Leah smiled.

"Leastwise we got boots," one of the others said. "I'd rather be walkin' with no clothes and boots, than with no boots and clothes."

Mike Rindell moved back through the formation of men until he came to Booker and Ebenezer.

"Sergeant Booker," he said. "I want you to know that I wish things were different."

"Cap'n, if wishes were wings, frogs wouldn't bump their asses everytime they jump," Booker said.

Despite the rancor in Booker's observation, Rindell smiled.

"No, I guess they wouldn't," he agreed. "What I'm trying to say is, I have a great deal of respect for a man who is a good soldier. I might think you're soldiering for the wrong side, but that doesn't lessen my respect for you. For either one of you."

"I got a plug in my pocket," Booker said. "Mind if I take it out for a chaw?"

"Go ahead."

Booker withdrew his plug of tobacco, offered it to Rindell, who declined, and to Ebenezer, who accepted. After Ebenezer took a chew, Booker took one, stuffed a few loose ends into his mouth, then returned the plug to his pocket. He started to say something, but the tobacco was in the way and he had to shift it in his mouth, then start again.

"The onliest thing that bothers me is, I wish it had been Chambers who was the spy instead of you. I'd taken a likin' to you, Cap'n. And I know the colonel liked you. In my book Chambers ain't worth a bucket of warm spit."

"Now you got two of 'em like that," Mills put in, having overheard the conversation.

"Ferguson?" Rindell asked.

"Yes, sir," Mills replied. "He's one sorry son of a bitch. It's funny, though. I would never have expected him to be a spy for the South."

"Why?" Booker asked. "Do you think men who love the South won't risk their lives for it?"

"Cap'n Ferguson holds no love for the South," Mills said. "And he's not a man of principle."

"Be that as it may, Sergeant, he is now fighting for the South," Rindell said.

"Yes, sir," Mills said. "I reckon he is."

A field correspondent for *Harper's Weekly* had once written that the railroad depot in Nashville was, in all probability, the busiest in the nation.

"Not even the rumbling of trains in New York's Grand Central Station can match the industriousness of the Nashville depot," the article read. "No fewer than twenty tracks, main lines, and sidings compose the rail yard. The building and platforms on the grounds are swelled with men and supplies going toward the front, and with prisoners, sick, and wounded being shuttled to the rear."

True to the correspondent's description, the Nashville depot was busy. Half a dozen switch engines chugged up and down the sidings, breaking strings of cars in one location, reassembling them in another. Scores of men stood or sat on the open platform, some resting on a pile of personal belongings, others leaning against stacks of military stores. On the street side of the depot, omnibuses and wagons stood, loading or unloading as their needs dictated. Across the street the two buildings that had once been the Railroad Hotel now served as headquarters buildings for the Union Army in Tennessee. The two buildings, one at a right angle to the other, sat atop a small hill so that the front was reached by a terrace of steps, ten in number, stretching the entire length of both buildings. Nearly as many men sat on those steps as were sitting on the depot platform.

The buildings were two stories high with second-floor casement windows, which opened out over the porch roof to allow a breeze. The same breeze that filled the muslin curtains in the open windows also caused the Stars and Stripes to ripple from the tall flagpole set in the open court between the buildings. In the distance, small and unthreatening, and therefore unmolested, a Confederate Stars and Bars fluttered from a crude staff someone had erected. In one of the offices off the main waiting room of the depot, Private Sickles, an army telegrapher, sat by his instrument, the key clacking noisily. The operator copied the message, then let out a low whistle.

"Sergeant, I reckon we'd better get this over to General Rosecrans right away," he said.

"What is it?"

"It's a message from the War Department in Washington. From Secretary Stanton," Sickles said. "You know that train we been expectin'? That Gold Train?"

"Yes."

"It says here the cap'n that's in charge of the men on that train's a spy. He done killed some woman in Washington."

The sergeant looked toward his telegrapher. "How do we know some Rebel hasn't tapped onto the line? Did you verify that message, Sickles?"

"Yes, sir, I did. It's real, all right."

The sergeant looked at the clock on the wall. "That train's supposed to be here in less than fifteen minutes," he said.

"What do you think we ought to do about it?"

"I think you're right. It should go over to General Rosecrans." He looked around. "Where's Dewey?"

"Don't you remember, Sarge? He had to go over to the other side of town to take a message to Major Fitzhugh."

"Damn. There's never anybody around when you need him." He sighed and put the message in an envelope. "All right. I reckon I better take it over myself."

"The lieutenant ain't gonna like that, Sarge," the telegrapher said. "You know how he wants a sergeant in here at all times."

"Yeah, and he wants messengers, too," the sergeant said. "But there ain't no messengers, and somebody's got to get this telegram over to General Rosecrans. Now, seein' as I don't know the code, I wouldn't be much good here all by myself if that thing started clackin' while I was gone, would I?"

"No, I reckon not," Sickles admitted.

"Then I'm going to take it over. I'll be right back."

The sergeant had been gone only two or three minutes when Private Sickles heard the machine start clacking again. It caught his attention immediately since it was not from one of his regular stations. He also found the hand of the telegrapher to be unfamiliar:

ATTENTION NASHVILLE STOP ATTENTION NASHVILLE STOP THIS IS AN EMERGENCY INTERCEPT STOP

Sickles leaned forward and tapped his key.

THIS IS NASHVILLE STOP WHO IS ON THIS LINE STOP

MY NAME IS RINDELL STOP I AM A FARADAY AGENT FOR THE WAR DEPARTMENT STOP URGENT THAT I SEND A MESSAGE TO GENERAL ROSECRANS STOP

Sickles stood up and, leaving the key, walked over to the window. He looked out to see if he his sergeant was returning yet. Behind him, he heard the key clacking again, snapping with the same sense of urgency.

"Damnation!" Sickles said aloud. "What am I supposed to do? I can't make a decision on this message. That's what we got sergeants and officers for."

Again the key clacked out an urgent request to be allowed to send a message.

Sickles sighed. It would not hurt to accept the message. He could pass it on to the sergeant and let the sergeant decide what to do. He reached down and fingered the key.

SEND YOUR MESSAGE STOP

The key clacked urgently as the message returned:

HALT THE GOLD TRAIN STOP HALT THE GOLD TRAIN STOP IT IS IN THE HANDS OF

THE REBELS STOP IT IS IN THE HANDS OF THE REBELS STOP SEND TRAIN FOR STRANDED PARTY NORTH OF NASHVILLE STOP

Sickles was no longer suspicious. He had just received a message that the captain in charge of the guard detail was a Rebel spy. Evidently that spy now had control of the train. Quickly, he sent a return message:

YOUR MESSAGE HAS BEEN RECEIVED STOP TRAIN WILL BE SENT STOP

Sickles tore the message off the pad, then hurried from his office to find the sergeant. The message was too important for him to wait. The key would have to stand by unattended.

Outside, hundreds of men were standing around waiting for transportation in one direction or another. They were packed onto the platform so close that it was difficult for Sickles to pick his way through them, and he had to go all the way around. It was no easier climbing the steps of the headquarters building, and then, when he finally did get inside, he had to talk his way past guards and clerks whose only job was to keep people out. Finally, he managed to get through to General Rosecrans's office, where he found his sergeant fuming quietly because he had just managed to get this far with his own message.

"What are you doing over here?" the sergeant asked. "Who's minding the key?"

"No one," Sickles admitted.

"What?"

"Sarge, you better look at this message, quick."

Sickles's sergeant read the message, then swore aloud.

"Dammit, Lieutenant!" the sergeant said, slamming his fist on the counter that separated the general's staff from those calling on him. "If you don't let me in to see Rosecrans this very minute, I'm going to let myself in, even if I have to go over you."

The lieutenant at the counter must have been fresh from Washington and had never heard a shot fired in anger. This administrative duty in Nashville was plainly as close to the fighting as he had ever been. But, although he had no experience, he did know enough about the army to understand that sergeants did not speak to lieutenants in such a fashion.

Standing up from his desk, he preened his mustache and faced the sergeant. "Sergeant, I'll thank you to keep a civil tongue in your head. I am an officer."

"You're an idiot," the sergeant said angrily, pushing open the little gate at one end of the counter.

"Colonel MacAphee, Colonel MacAphee!" the lieutenant screamed, his voice rising in pitch as he grew angrier.

The colonel, unlike his lieutenant, had been in more than a dozen battles, large and small. When he heard his lieutenant's high-pitched shout, he came out of his own office and looked around.

"What's going on out here?" he bellowed.

"This man has forced himself in here," the lieutenant said. "I tried to tell him to wait his turn, that you or General Rosecrans would see him in the proper order."

"Is that true, Sergeant?"

"Yes, sir," the sergeant said. He held up the two messages he had. "But, by God, Colonel, if we don't act right now, it's too late. The Rebels have the Gold Train, and it's coming through here in about five minutes."

"God's thunder, Lieutenant! Did he tell you this?" Colonel MacAphee roared.

"Yes, sir," the lieutenant answered meekly. "But there were others in front of him."

"How in heaven's name did you get your commission, Lieutenant? You don't have sense enough to pour piss from a boot with instructions printed on the heel. Come on, Sergeant," MacAphee said as he pushed open the gate and strode toward the doorway. "Let's see if we can get that train stopped."

"If we can get to the switch in time, we can throw the train over onto one of the sidings," Sickles suggested, following after the sergeant and the colonel.

"Good idea!" the colonel called back.

The three men clumped down the stairs, then ran out the front door. With the sergeant yelling "Make way!" the three men moved through the body of waiting passengers like Moses parting the sea. They ran across the road, over the depot platform, then down toward the main switch.

"We ain't gonna make it!" Sickles shouted. "There's the train!"

Just as Sickles pointed to it, the Gold Train entered the depot yard from the north. Even if they had not known of the message, they would have suspected something was wrong the moment they saw this train. Whereas most trains entered the yard at a speed of no more than five miles per hour, this train was barreling down the track at high speed. Long before the three men reached the switch that would have diverted the train to one of the sidings, it had already cleared that junction and was coming into the depot.

Many of the waiting passengers had wandered down onto the track, and when they saw the speed at which the train was approaching, they had to hurry to get out of the way. They hurled invectives at the engineer.

"Slow down!"

"What the hell?"

"Who does he think he is?"

The engineer blew his whistle, more in warning than greeting, and the train rushed past them at forty miles an hour, smoke and steam trailing back in long wisps, great driver wheels pounding at the rails, sparks flying from the firebox. The blast of air and noise from its passing shook the buildings themselves, and the windows of the cars streamed by so fast as to be almost one long blur.

There were men, dressed in Union uniforms, standing on the platforms between the cars. They waved and smiled at the startled crowd by the tracks, and then the train roared on through until, a few moments later, nothing was left of it but a wisp of smoke on the horizon.

The Rebels had gotten away.

Chapter 9

MIKE RINDELL TAPPED INTO THE TELEGRAPH WIRES. COLOnel MacAphee sent a train for them, which arrived within half an hour. As soon as it reached the depot, Rindell hurried to MacAphee's office, where he studied numerous railroad maps of Nashville and the surrounding area and discussed the robbery and the kidnapping with the general.

"They can't be more than twenty miles south," Rindell observed, pointing to the wall map. "Actually, I'd be surprised if they made it that far. It's been a while since they took on water, and since they didn't stop here, that has to be critical. Where's the next place south they can get it?"

MacAphee raised his finger to the map and said, "Murfreesboro, if they took the Nashville and Georgia . . . Franklin, if they took the Central Alabama."

"I suggest that you send wires to those two places, sir. Tell them to deny water to any train until it is thoroughly searched."

"Good idea," MacAphee agreed. He nodded toward the signal sergeant, who took the message into the other room for Sickles to dispatch.

"You say they have General Mayhew's wife on board the train?"

"Yes, sir," Rindell said. "They moved her into the baggage car with the gold."

"Poor woman," MacAphee said. He rubbed his hand through his thinning hair. "Well, we've got to get her back."

A moment later the signal sergeant returned and reported to the general. "Sickles sent the messages, sir. He got through all the way to Murfreesboro on the Nashville and Georgia Line. The train hasn't been through there, yet."

MacAphee nodded. "Good. What about Franklin?"

"He couldn't raise Franklin or anyone else on the Central Alabama line," the sergeant said. "The wire's down."

MacAphee looked over at Rindell, who was still studying the map very closely.

"Now what?" MacAphee asked.

"Tyreen must have cut the wire," Rindell suggested.

"He could have," MacAphee admitted. "But the fact that it's down doesn't necessarily mean anything. It goes down pretty often anyway. It's just our luck it's down today."

"Colonel MacAphee, if you were Tyreen, which track would you take to get out of here?"

"This one," Colonel MacAphee said, pointing to the Nashville and Georgia. "The one going toward Murfreesboro."

"Why?"

"Well, his base is in northern Georgia, isn't it? This track is the shortest way to get there. It also will return him to his own lines quicker than the other one."

"By the other one, you mean the Central Alabama," Rindell said.

"Well, yes, of course," MacAphee said. He pointed to another set of tracks. "This third track is just the

Kingston Springs spur. It only goes about thirty miles due west, then comes to a dead end at Kingston Springs. And, as you can see, there are no spurs leading from it, so once you get on that track, there's nothing you can do but turn around and come right back here."

"Beg pardon, Colonel," the signal sergeant interrupted. "But I told Private Sickles to send a wire to Belleview. They've disabled that water tower, too."

"Belleview?" Rindell asked.

"That's here," the colonel said, pointing to a little spot on the Kingston Spur. "It's the only water on the entire spur."

"Good idea," Rindell said.

"Seems like a waste," Colonel MacAphee said. "Like I told you, even if he did take that line, there's no place he could go."

"Sir," Rindell said, turning toward the colonel, "do you know much about the game of baseball?"

MacAphee's brow furrowed. "I've seen the men playing it in camps."

"There's a saying in baseball, sir, that one should have all the bases covered. That's the way I feel about Tyreen. When you're dealing with a man like him, you should have all the bases covered. Now with the water being denied on the Nashville and Georgia, and on the Kingston Spur, that leaves only the Central Alabama. And the wire on the Central Alabama has been cut."

MacAphee held up his finger and wagged it back and forth. "Uh, uh. I didn't say cut . . . I said down. There's a difference."

"Nevertheless, it is down, and that is the only 'base' left uncovered. Colonel, I have no choice but to go down that track and see if I can find him."

"You're going to chase him?"

"Damn right, I am," Rindell answered.

The colonel rubbed his chin. "It might be a wild goose chase."

"I know Tyreen, sir, and I know that he's going to

do what we least expect him to do. If we expect him to take the shortest route back home, he's going to take the longest. And the fact that there is no telegraph service along that route just strengthens my belief. Anyway, what have we got to lose? If Murfreesboro does what we ask, there's no way the train can get any farther than that, even if they did go that way."

MacAphee was silent for a moment, and then he said, "All right. You seem to be representing the War Department in this, and I'm sure General Rosecrans would want me to do whatever I can to help you. What do you need?"

Mike Rindell smiled with relief. "I need the fastest engine in the yard. Also, a tender and a car for the twenty volunteers I'll be taking with me."

"Sergeant, see to it," MacAphee ordered. When the signal sergeant had left the room again, MacAphee cleared his throat and said, "Uh, Mr. Rindell, you know this man Tyreen pretty well, don't you?"

"Yes, sir, pretty well," Rindell agreed.

"What kind of man is he?"

"He's a good man, Colonel. He's the kind of man we'd like to have on our side," Rindell answered without hesitation.

"Will he harm the woman?"

"Not intentionally. But neither will he let her presence stop him from putting up a fight if he's caught."

The colonel paced to the window and, looking out, asked, "And do you anticipate a fight?"

"As I said, sir, he's a good man. He won't just give up."

"Then by all means . . . please, do be careful." MacAphee turned toward Rindell. "If anything happens to the general's wife while she is in my jurisdiction . . ." He let the sentence hang. "Oh, by the way, I wouldn't go down there in that uniform if I were you."

Rindell looked down at the gray tunic he was

wearing and chuckled. "No, I guess not. I forgot about it. Have you got any suggestions?"

"Because of my dealings with civilian suppliers, I have the authority to appoint anyone to the rank of captain of the quartermaster corps, for a period not to exceed sixty days," MacAphee offered. "Not a very glamorous position, I admit, but it would be the fastest way to put you in a Union officer's uniform and make it legal."

Rindell nodded. "I accept, as long as it can be done quickly. And as long as it's temporary. When this mission is over, I intend to return to Washington for my next assignment. I can't see spending the rest of the war in Nashville, counting blankets."

The colonel laughed. "I'll draw up the commission specifically for the duration of this mission then." Pointing to the warehouse, he added, "There are fifty thousand uniforms in that building over there, so it shouldn't take you long to find what you need. By the time you are dressed, we should have your train ready."

Five minutes later, as Mike Rindell, wearing the uniform and insignia of a captain of quartermaster, stood alongside the track, a special train was drawn up for his use. Beside him was Leah Saunders, who had waited for him outside of Colonel MacAphee's office.

The special train and the soldiers about to board it drew the attention of everyone present, and a great crowd gathered to look at it. Those workers in the yard who knew railroad equipment agreed that they had selected the fastest engine in the depot and one of the fastest in the country. Not only that, it was one of the most beautiful. Named the *Union,* the engine had been built by the Grant Locomotive Works in 1862. All the fittings and trimmings were of polished brass. The boiler was painted forest green; the cab, crimson with gilt lettering. With four wheels per side and high driver wheels, it had such a rakish appearance that, even when sitting at rest, she looked fast. Nothing was attached to the engine except the tender and one box car.

Rindell and Leah stood alongside the *Union* as tendrils of steam slipped from the cylinders and drifted away.

"Cap'n, I got the volunteers, sir," Sergeant Mills said, saluting him.

Rindell smiled. "I was hoping you'd be one of them, Sergeant Mills."

"No way I'm going to miss this," Mills exclaimed.

"What is this?" one of the volunteers asked. "We're bein' led by a quartermaster officer?"

"Be careful what you say, soldier," Sergeant Mills reprimanded him as the men climbed into the boxcar. "You'll never go into battle with a better officer."

"You seem to have won a convert," Leah said quietly.

"Yes. I hope I live up to his expectations," Rindell said. "You ready? You and I will ride in the engine."

"Wait a minute, Captain," Colonel MacAphee spoke up. "You don't mean to take that woman with you, do you?"

"Yes, of course I do," Rindell answered.

"I'm afraid I can't allow that."

"You can't allow it?" Leah questioned. "Excuse me, Colonel, but what have you to do with it? I'm working for Secretary Stanton and the War Department."

"That may be, miss, but I'm responsible for the safety of all the civilians in my area. And I won't be—"

"I'm afraid it's quite out of your hands, Colonel," Rindell interrupted, helping Leah climb into the engine. "She's going."

"Now, just you hold on there," MacAphee sputtered. "You are a captain and I—"

Rindell, who had climbed into the engine just behind Leah, now turned and looked down through the window at MacAphee and interrupted his blustering. "Colonel, you've been a big help so far. Don't get in the way now. If you need verification of what we're doing, wire the War Department. Like the lady told you, she is here under Secretary Stanton's orders. And I don't think the secretary of war is going to appreciate being bothered with this. After all, he has given his orders once, and that should be enough for someone in his position. His orders shouldn't be questioned over and over again."

Colonel MacAphee was not exactly sure how the conversation had turned to where it looked as if he was questioning the secretary's orders. Nevertheless, that was what he was hearing from Rindell's lips. He started to protest again to explain his position. Then, realizing it would do no good and that he was just wasting valuable time, he held his tongue. Instead, he smiled and shook his head.

"All right, Captain. If you know what you're doing, I'll leave it up to you."

"Thank you, sir," Rindell said. "Now, I'd appreciate it if you would signal the switchmen farther up the yard. Have the switches set for the Central Alabama line. We're going through at full speed."

Even as Colonel MacAphee was answering, Rindell reached up and jerked on the whistle cord. A second later the engineer had the throttle open all the way, and the locomotive, considerably lightened of its normal load, was able to accelerate rapidly. It was nimble and quick, and nearly everyone in the yard watched in fascination as the abbreviated train flew past them, already at top speed by the time it crossed the outer switches.

As the train raced south out of the city, Leah sat on a little wooden bench, out of the way of the engineer and the fireman. The latter was working furiously, feeding wood into the firebox to maintain the steam pressure needed to drive the train. The engine clattered over a trestle and across a road, then ran parallel for a short time with a residential street. Leah looked out at the houses with their neat lawns and gardens. In the backyard of one house she saw a woman hanging clothes out to dry. The woman seemed oblivious to the train passing by at such great speed . . . oblivious to the war and to the battles raging all over the South. She was self-contained in her own little world.

The scene of peaceful domesticity in the midst of a nation at war touched Leah more than she wanted to admit. For an instant she wished she could trade places with the woman at the clothesline. She played with the idea, losing herself in that thought. It would be so peaceful and pleasant to be concerned with getting the wash dry, and as she thought of it, she could almost smell the sun on the laundry, feel the clothes in her hands.

What if?

What if she were a housewife and she were married to Mike Rindell? What if he were a banker, or lawyer, or merchant? What if they lived in that house . . . right there . . . white, two story, with a green roof?

As the train hurtled on, Leah stared sightlessly at the window. In her mind's eye she saw the house. A magnolia tree and two elms stood in the front yard. A flowering dogwood and redbud were in the side yard, and a mulberry was in the back, along with a neat barn and well-constructed outhouse. She saw a garden, where she could see herself raising vegetables, and a rootcellar where she could keep them, once canned. She looked at the top floor, at the room on the southeast corner. It had several windows for the morning sun and would be perfect for a nursery.

The engine passed over several switch plates, and it jerked and swerved so sharply that Leah was jolted from her musing. Her eyes, as well as her thoughts, returned to the inside of the engine cab, where she saw not soft clothes and spring sun but steel plates and brass fittings. The firebox was roaring, the engine gauges were quivering, the steam was hissing, and she could feel the powerful throb of the piston rods and driver wheels underneath.

"Faster!" Rindell was shouting. "Faster! We've got to catch up with them!"

"We're doin' sixty now, Cap'n!" the engineer shouted back. "We put on any more steam pressure and the boiler's gonna bust!"

Leah looked out again, but it was too late. The house was no longer in view. They were through the city now, and every minute that passed put Nashville and the little two-story house another mile behind. Her own fleeting thoughts of domesticity had flown a million miles away.

They reached Franklin within thirty minutes after leaving Nashville. Rindell was leaning out the window on the left-hand side of the engine when he saw that the spout had been lowered from the water tower. He took that to mean that a train had just come through and had taken on water.

"They've been here!" he shouted. "They've already taken on water. How's ours?"

"We have enough for another hour!" the engineer called back.

"Then don't stop!" Rindell ordered. "Taking on water had to slow Tyreen down. I'm sure he's just in front of us. We'll keep going!"

As they pounded through the Franklin depot at top speed, they attracted attention. Soldiers and civilians, men and women, rushed toward the track to watch the train pass. Many had never seen anything moving this fast, and the sight thrilled them. Suddenly Rindell's engineer saw that a switch engine was on the track in front of them. He hauled back on the brake lever and pulled on his whistle cord, blowing it as long and as loud as he could.

In the little switch engine, the engineer must have realized that his only hope of avoiding the onrushing train was to speed up and get out of the way. His speed increased, but the *Union* was closing on him so fast that everyone in the *Union* cab, as well as those alongside the tracks, knew they were about to crash.

As the bystanders were mouthing prayers, a quick-thinking switchman ran to the track just in front of the yard's switch engine and threw the switch bar, then impatiently waved the little engine through. Those watching held their breath as they measured the speed of closure of the *Union* against that of the switch engine and the shunt. Then the little engine left the main track and scooted off to one side.

The instant the yard engine cleared the pullout, the switchman slammed the lever over again, just seconds before the *Union* whipped by, still on the main track. The engineer blew his whistle in thanks and pushed open the throttle again, and everyone in the Franklin depot looked on in fascination as the speeding locomotive continued south, almost as if nothing had happened.

Forty-five minutes later the *Union* approached the town of Pulaski. The engineer slowed the train and looked around at Rindell.

"Captain Rindell, if you plan to go any farther, we're gonna have to take on water here. There's not another tower till we reach Decatur, and like as not that's in the hands of the secessionists."

"All right," Rindell agreed. "Go ahead and do it. I'll see if the telegraph wires are open yet."

The train pulled into the yard with its bell clanging and the wheels squeaking as the brakes were applied. The door to the boxcar was crowded with Sergeant Mills's volunteers, looking out onto the little town.

"That's strange," the engineer observed as the engine coasted to a stop under the water tower.

"What's strange?" Rindell asked.

"Normally Pete is out here pulling the spout down by this time."

"This is a special train," Rindell said. "He wasn't expecting us."

"That's true," the engineer agreed. "Tony, reckon you're gonna have to climb up there and pull the thing down yourself," he said to the fireman.

"All right," Tony replied. The fireman climbed out of the cab, and even as the engine coasted to a stop, he had the valve open and the spout down. He pulled the rope, and water began gushing down into the tank.

"Cap'n, is it all right if the boys stretch their legs?" Mills called up.

"Give them a stretch, Mills," Rindell said. "I'm going to walk over to the station and check on the telegraph wires."

"I'll go with you," Leah offered, and she climbed down from the engine to join Rindell.

The water tower was about fifty yards from the depot, and as they walked down the track, Rindell looked around the little train station. Unlike the depot in Nashville, where many tracks and sidings made the area a vast railroad yard, there were only two tracks here, the main track and one siding. Three boxcars sat on the siding, their doors open and the wind whistling through them. The depot platform, like the depot itself, appeared to be totally deserted.

"Where is everyone?" Rindell asked, standing next to the track.

"Maybe you're just not used to such a small town," Leah suggested.

"That's just what I mean. In small towns like this, you'd think almost everyone would be interested enough in what's going on to come down to the depot and look. You don't see a train like ours coming through here every day. Isn't anyone curious?"

There was a loud, banging noise, and Leah jumped and reached out to grab Rindell. The banging repeated, and Rindell looked up to see a window shutter on the top of the depot building banging open and shut in the wind. That same gust of wind then whipped a piece of tin across the track and blew it up against one of the empty cars, where it made a clattering sound before freeing itself from the car, then tumbling on into the town.

Leah laughed. "I'm sorry I jumped. I got scared by a window shutter."

Rindell suddenly stopped and looked around. Leah stopped with him.

"Mike, what is it?"

"Look down this street," Rindell said, pointing. The main street of the town crossed the railroad at right angles, and they were just now even with it. This put them in position to have a clear view of the buildings on both sides of the road.

Leah looked in the direction he indicated.

"I don't see anything," she said.

"That's just it," Rindell said. "There's something wrong here."

"Mike, look!" Leah suddenly shouted, pointing to the depot.

A man wearing the uniform of a Confederate captain had just come out of the depot and was standing on the platform.

"Yankee. I expect you and the girl better stay right there," the Rebel captain said.

Rindell grabbed Leah's arm and pulled her back. "Come on. We have to get to the train!"

As they started running, more Confederate soldiers appeared. They had been hiding all this time, and now they popped up from everywhere, from ditches and from behind buildings and bushes. Some had even been inside the empty boxcars.

"It's an ambush! Get the train moving!" Rindell shouted.

From behind them, Rindell heard a series of popping sounds, then the whistle and buzz of minie balls. The soldiers were shooting at them.

Sergeant Mills and half a dozen of his men started running toward Rindell and Leah. When Mills gave the order, his men stopped running, then raised their rifles to their shoulders. Another ripple of gunfire came from behind Rindell, and he saw two of Sergeant Mills's men go down. Mills gave the order to fire, and there was a flash of light and gush of smoke from their rifles, and Rindell heard the minie balls whistling by in the opposite direction.

"Run, Captain! Run, miss!" Mills shouted.

The soldiers, having fired one volley, picked up their comrades and started back to the train with them. By now Rindell and Leah were even with them.

"Are these Tyreen's men, Cap'n?" Mills asked, as they ran to the train.

"No. I've never seen them before," Rindell answered.

"Where the blazes did they all come from?" Mills asked. "I thought we were still in Union territory."

By now more of Rindell's guard detail had arrived, and they loosed a second volley, which managed to keep the Rebels back. After taking a few more steps, they reached the train.

"Get aboard!" Rindell shouted. "We're getting out of here!"

Mills and his troops climbed back into the boxcar, while Rindell and Leah clambered up to the engine.

"Let's go! Straight ahead!" Rindell said.

He had no sooner gotten the words out of his mouth than he heard the thunder of a twelve-pounder cannon. The ball whistled overhead, missing the engine by several feet but hitting in between the tracks a few yards ahead. The ball knocked one of the rails loose.

"Captain, look!" the engineer shouted.

"Damn!" Rindell replied. "All right, we'll have to go back through them!"

The engineer threw the Johnson bar into reverse, and the engine began backing up. Rindell heard a ripple of gunfire from the boxcar, and he knew that his men were shooting at the Rebels. When he looked up, he saw that some of his men had taken positions in the tender itself and were firing from the woodpile.

Rindell pulled his pistol, and standing on the

platform between the engine and tender, he started shooting as well.

Just then a bullet came through the open window of the engine and hit a steam gauge. A gush of steam filled the cab, and the fireman let out a yelp of pain, but working quickly, he was able to twist the valve and shut off the flow of steam. Another bullet hit the cab's ceiling, then rattled around inside.

Rindell saw that one of the Rebels who was doing the most damage had taken a commanding position atop the depot building. As they backed up to the depot, Rindell took slow and careful aim at the Rebel on the roof, squeezed the trigger, and was rewarded by seeing the man grab his chest and pitch forward. His rifle slid down the roof of the depot, hit the brick platform below, and broke into two pieces at the small of the stock. The Rebel soldier slid down the roof behind his rifle, also falling to the brick platform, where he lay motionless.

"Hold it! Stop the train!" Rindell shouted. "They're throwing the switch to send us onto the siding!"

Then, even as the engineer was stopping the train, Rindell saw Sergeant Mills jump from the boxcar and charge toward the switch. The two Rebel soldiers standing there picked up their rifles, but a murderous fire from the Union men in the train dropped them before they could shoot. Mills made it to the switch and turned it back so the train would be able to stay on the main line. Even over the noise of battle and the train, Rindell heard his men cheer as Mills started back.

"Hurry, Mills, hurry!" Rindell urged, but his exhortations were in vain, for Mills suddenly pitched forward, then lay beside the track, his arms stretched in front of him. Even from the cab of the engine Rindell could see that Sergeant Mills was dead, the back of his head blown away by a minie ball.

"Oh, Mike, he . . ." Leah said, and she turned her head away as tears started down her cheeks. Rindell put one arm around her to comfort her, while with the other hand he continued to fire his pistol at the Rebels.

By now the train was traveling at a fair rate of speed. They passed Sergeant Mills's prostrate body and the bodies of several Rebel soldiers. As the train rolled by the depot and the empty boxcars on the siding, a dozen Confederate soldiers on both sides of the tracks fired another volley. The cannon roared a second time, and the ball smashed into the side of the tender, tearing a large, gaping hole in the car, then smashing around inside, turning a pile of wood into kindling sticks.

The *Union* passed all the way through the station and out the north side, the same way it had arrived a few minutes earlier. As the depot began to recede in the distance, a dozen or more Rebels, frustrated at letting the train get away, chased them down the track, finally kneeling and firing one more volley at them. The cannon, too, loosed a last round, this time firing an explosive shell that burst in the air just over the train and rained shrapnel down on them, but doing no real damage.

Within a matter of minutes the train was five miles north of town, passing through quiet meadows, peaceful farms and silent woods. Rindell ordered the engine stopped since they were out of danger.

The train came to a halt between two open fields, with only the cracking and popping of cooling gearboxes and venting of steam from the safety valve disturbing the serenity of the pastoral scene. Rindell had specifically chosen this place to stop because there was no chance of more Rebels being in position to ambush them.

"Leah, check on the men," he said. "See how many wounded we have, and if you can do anything for them, do it. I'm going to see if the telegraph line is open back to Nashville."

"All right," Leah agreed.

While Rindell climbed the telegraph pole next to the track, Leah walked back to the boxcar. When she looked inside, she saw that three men had been placed to one side. They were lying perfectly still, their hats pulled down over their faces.

"They're dead, ma'am," one of the soldiers said. "Them and Sergeant Mills. Makes four we lost."

"What about wounds?" Leah asked.

"Billy over there got shot in the ass—uh, hip, ma'am."

"Help me into the car." Leah stretched her hand up, and the soldier pulled her onto the car. She walked over to look at Billy. She recognized him as one of the soldiers who had been constantly engaged in a poker game during the trip from Washington. She knelt beside him.

"Lord, miss, you ain't gonna take a look at my wound, are you?" Billy asked. "It's . . . it's in an indelicate place," he added.

"I shall examine it with as much modesty as possible," Leah said. "Can you turn over, or does it hurt too much?"

"I can turn over," Billy said. With an effort, he rolled to one side, displaying the wound. It was an ugly, red gash, cut deep into his flesh. Someone had stuffed a uniform jacket against it to stop the bleeding.

"Here, we can do better than that," Leah said. She reached under her dress and began tugging on her slip. A moment later she stepped out of it, then taking away the uniform jacket, replaced it with the white cotton that had been her undergarment.

"Yes'm," Billy said. "That feels better. Thank you, ma'am."

"Leah," Rindell called. When she looked around, she saw that he was standing on the ground next to the open car door. "We're going back to Nashville."

"Did you get through?"

"Yes," Rindell said. "The wire has been replaced."

"Cap'n, you reckon we'll run into any more Rebs between here and Nashville?" one of the soldiers asked.

"No," Rindell said. "That was General Nathan Bedford Forrest's men we encountered. According to the news I just got over the wire, they captured Pulaski this morning, but that was as far north as they came."

Rindell helped Leah down, and they walked back to the engine. The engineer and fireman were standing alongside the tender, looking at the hole the cannon ball had put in the side.

"Look at that," the engineer said. "It went through two inches of steel like it was paper."

"We can be glad it didn't hit the boiler," Rindell said, recalling Tyreen's Raiders and the stories they told of "busting" engines with cannon fire. "By the way, how much water did we get?"

"We got a fair amount," the fireman said. "Enough to get us back to Franklin, where we can get some more."

"All right, let's go back," Rindell said.

The engineer, fireman, Rindell, and Leah climbed back into the cab. Leah gave Rindell the report on the men who had been killed and on Billy, who had been wounded.

"I didn't get much of a chance to know Sergeant Mills," Rindell said. "But I liked what I knew of him."

"He was a good man," Leah agreed.

"And he died for nothing," Rindell said in a frustrated tone. The train began creeping down the tracks.

"What do you mean?"

"I mean Tyreen didn't even come down this track. I wired Franklin . . . we're the only train to come through besides the scheduled morning run. If I hadn't been in such an all-fired hurry, I could have stopped and asked when we came through. But I was so sure that Tyreen was just ahead of us, I didn't want to take the time to stop and inquire."

"Mike, you did what you thought was best under

the circumstances," Leah said. "You had good reason to believe Tyreen was in front of us."

"Tell that to Mills," Rindell said.

She put her hand on his jaw. "Mike, Sergeant Mills was killed because he risked his life to turn the switch that let us escape. He may have saved the lives of everyone on this train, and in my book, that doesn't make his death a waste. He died a hero's death. If I had the authority, I'd put him in for one of those medals Congress has authorized, the Medal of Honor."

Mike Rindell held out his arm and looked at the federal blue of his jacket. "Well, I guess I do have the authority," he said. "And I'll see to it that the medal is given to his family." He sighed, then added with self-condemning sarcasm, "I'm sure it'll keep them warm on a cold night."

Leah leaned against him and let him put his arm around her, trying to comfort the man the best way she could. She could tell from the tension in his body and the way he held himself, though, that there was little that could comfort him at this moment.

The *Union* backed all the way to Franklin, where in addition to taking on water it also used the turntable to turn around, thus allowing them to complete the return trip to Nashville with the engine going forward.

Once they had arrived and the dead and wounded had been taken care of, Mike Rindell visited Colonel MacAphee's office and gave him a complete report of what happened.

"Of course," MacAphee agreed, when Rindell told him of Sergeant Mills's heroics. "I'll be glad to endorse your recommendation for the Medal of Honor for Sergeant Mills. I've never heard of anyone deserving it more."

Rindell leaned against the long table in MacAphee's office and studied the map on the wall before him. "Colonel," he said. "Where the hell did Tyreen go? He couldn't just disappear into thin air. That train is out there somewhere."

"I don't know," MacAphee said. "All I know is he never showed up in Murfreesboro, and he never showed up in Franklin."

"Tyreen, I knew you were good," Rindell said quietly. "But I didn't know you were this good."

Chapter 10

"How much longer, Mr. Engineer?" Lieutenant Colonel Jebediah Tyreen asked as he scratched his chin with the hook at the end of his left arm. The Gold Train was stopped, and Tyreen, Major Blackie Chambers, and Captain Gerald Ferguson were standing outside it, looking up atop the engine, where the engineer was sitting.

"At the rate we're goin', it'll be at least another half hour before we have enough water," the engineer answered.

Even as he spoke, the fireman, who was sitting beside the engineer on top of the engine, took a bucket that was handed up to him by one of Tyreen's soldiers and poured its contents into the tank.

After the bucket was emptied, the men passed it back along the line to the last soldier, who dipped it into Bear Creek, then passed it back up. When it reached the fireman, he poured into the tank again.

"What I can't figure is why all the water had been drained out of the tower back in Belleview," Major

Chambers said. "There wasn't a soul around, but the water was all over the ground, just as if someone had purposely dumped it."

"Someone did," Tyreen said. "Unless I miss my guess, Mike Rindell wired ahead to have the water denied to us on all the routes out of Nashville."

Major Chambers shook his head as he propped a foot on the step to the cab. "Colonel, I don't mind telling you that I'm not sorry to see Rindell turn out the way he did. Unlike you, I never had any particular fondness for the man. Also, unlike you, I don't credit him with the intelligence you are so ready to concede. I can't believe he is quick-witted enough to think of such a thing."

"He was quick-witted enough to cut his car loose from the rest of the train," Tyreen reminded him.

"Even so," Gerald Ferguson put in, joining the conversation, "that would make it even more difficult to believe Rindell could be behind dumping all the water. The only way he had into Nashville was to walk. Why, I wouldn't be surprised if he was just now getting there."

"And I wouldn't be surprised if he hadn't already commandeered a train and started out after us," Tyreen said.

"So is that why you decided to take this track?" Chambers asked. "Because you were afraid of Rindell?"

"Exactly."

Ferguson rubbed his hands together and looked at the line of soldiers pouring water into the engine. "Yes, well, I'll give you this, Colonel. He certainly won't think of coming out on this track to find us. It doesn't go anywhere." He looked at Tyreen. "Which brings up the next question. What good has it done us? We got away from them this time, but have you figured out how to get out of here? There's no way without going right back through the Nashville depot again."

"That's just what we're going to do," Tyreen said, looking off into the distance.

"Oh, I get it," Ferguson said. "We're going to wait until nightfall, then sneak back through. Is that it?"

"That'll never work," Chambers put in quickly.

"Why not?" Ferguson asked.

"You try to take this train through that yard at night . . . as jumpy as all the guards are, they'll open up on us for sure."

"Gentlemen, we won't be going through the yard at night," Tyreen replied. "We're going through in broad daylight."

Ferguson smiled. "Is this some of the Southern bravado we've read about in the Northern papers?" he asked. "It would be even more suicidal to go through in broad daylight than it would be to go through at night."

"Not if they don't know who we are," Tyreen said. He smiled. "Trust me, gentlemen."

When the boiler tank was filled with water, Tyreen told the engineer to fire it up. He, Chambers, and Ferguson climbed into the cab with the engineer and fireman, and Tyreen gave his orders.

"You will recall, Mr. Engineer, a small siding we passed on the way out here? I believe the place was called Vaughan."

"Yeah, I know the place," the engineer said.

"There were four or five freight cars sitting on that siding. We are going to return to Vaughan and switch the cars we are pulling for those cars."

"Hey," Chambers said, brightening. "That might work. We'll go right back through Nashville looking like a freight train."

"You think just gettin' rid of the varnish is all you need? That won't do you any good," the fireman mumbled.

"Charlie, hush up," the engineer hissed.

"What do you mean it won't do any good?" Tyreen asked.

"Nothin'. I didn't mean nothin' by it."

"What's varnish?" Ferguson asked.

"Varnish is what trainmen call passengers cars," Tyreen answered. He stroked his chin whiskers with his hook and studied the facial expressions of the engineer and fireman. Then he laughed softly. "You're right," he said.

"What?" Chambers asked. "What do you mean? Colonel Tyreen, I thought it sounded like a damn good idea."

"I like it, too," Ferguson agreed.

"Gentlemen, that's because you don't understand the term varnish."

"Beg your pardon, sir?"

Tyreen chuckled. "Meaning you aren't trainmen." He pointed to the engineer and fireman. "These men are, and they just made me realize something I had almost forgotten."

"What's that?" Ferguson asked.

"When the average person looks at a train, he sees only the makeup of the train—what kind of cars are being pulled, whether it's passenger or freight. But a trainman, a real trainman, sees the engine and tender, and no matter what you do to the rest of the train, he would still recognize it. What I think Charlie has just pointed out to us is that the trainmen in the Nashville depot would recognize us immediately, whether we were pulling freight cars or not."

"Damn," Ferguson said. "So we're stuck out here?"

"Not quite," Tyreen said. "Thanks to Charlie, I have an idea."

"Charlie," the engineer said. "You have a big mouth."

"Sorry," the fireman mumbled.

"Take us to Vaughan, Mr. Engineer," Tyreen ordered.

At Vaughan the baggage, kitchen, and passenger cars were shunted off to the siding. As the engineer was making the switch, one of Tyreen's men came up to him and pointed to the string of freight cars sitting on the siding.

"Colonel, be you aimin' to hook up to them there cars?"

"Yes," Tyreen said. "I want us to look like a freight

train." He looked at the soldier and saw him shake his head. "Why do you ask? Is there any reason why I shouldn't?"

"Well, sir, I ain't nothin' but a private, an' I ain't got no business tellin' a colonel his business, but . . ."

"Get on with it, man," Tyreen urged. "If you know something that will affect the success or failure of this mission, it's your duty to bring it to my attention."

"Well, sir, before the war I worked up here as a engine wiper for the Nashville and Memphis. I recall these very same cars was in the depot then, and they was brought out here to get 'em out of the way."

"Out of the way? Why?"

"Why, Colonel, ever'one of 'em's got a flat spot on one of the wheels . . . some of 'em got two or three flat wheels."

"I see," Tyreen said. He looked at the private who had brought him the information. "Can they be moved?"

"Yes, sir, they can be moved. They was brought out here all right. That is, iffen the wheelbearings ain't plumb dry of grease. They gonna be noisy critters though, banging and bumping around. And you're not gonna be able to go very fast with 'em."

"We won't have to go very fast," Tyreen said. "After all, we are going to be a slow freight. By the way, would you check the wheel bearings for me . . . let me know just how dry they might be?"

"Yes, sir," The private started toward the freight cars, then stopped and looked back toward Tyreen. "Iffen they is dry, Colonel, you ain't gonna get as far as Nashville with 'em before they seize up on you."

Tyreen looked over at the shining passenger cars they had just dropped off. "Tell me, son," he said. "Would it be possible to take some of the grease from the wheelbearings of those cars and transfer it to the freight cars?"

The soldier smiled broadly and nodded enthusiastically. "Why, yes, sir, it sure would be," he said. "I might need to have a few fellers get their hands dirty, but it can be done."

"Good. Do it."

"Yes, sir."

A few minutes later half a dozen of Tyreen's men were cleaning out grease from the boxes and bearings of the passenger car wheels and applying it to the wheelbearings of the old freight cars. While that was going on, the most artistic of Tyreen's men was changing the number on the engine and the lettering on the tender with some oil paints Julia Mayhew had packed with her luggage. It had been U.S.M.R., for United States Military Railroad. Tyreen had it changed to read N & C for Nashville and Chattanooga. He also had the diamond top removed from the train's smokestack.

The private who had pointed out the necessity of greasing the wheel bearings came up to stand beside Tyreen. He looked at the work being done on the engine. "Colonel, would you mind a suggestion?" he asked.

"Not at all," Tyreen replied. "If it's as good as the other one."

The private rubbed his cheek, leaving a small grease smear, and he pointed to the engine.

"Well, sir, iffen you look there, you see a engine that's all nice an' shiny. I mean, that there was a special train the Yanks put on the line, and it was carryin' a general's wife, so they wanted it to be particular nice. Now, look at freight cars we're hookin' up to it. Them cars is old an' rusted-out lookin'."

"I see," Tyreen said. "What you're telling me is the cars don't go with the engine."

"No, sir, they sure don't. And changin' the number and the stack ain't gonna help much, neither."

"All right," Tyreen said. "Sergeant . . ."

"I'm a private, sir."

"You're a sergeant now."

The newly promoted sergeant beamed proudly.

"Get all the men together," Tyreen said. "I don't care how you do it, but I want that engine looking as bad as the cars."

"Yes, sir."

A few minutes later, with all the wheel bearings newly greased, the string of freight cars was connected to the engine. Then the raiders attacked the engine, scraping the boiler and tender with sand and rocks and smearing it with grease. The polished brass fittings were pulled off, and someone cracked the glass over the headlamp.

The engineer stood by helplessly as his beautiful engine was systematically attacked. He felt tears come to his eyes, and he turned away so that he would not have to watch. Suddenly he felt a hand on his shoulder, and when he looked up, he saw Colonel Tyreen. The expression on Tyreen's face was almost as pained as his own.

"Colonel, look at what your men's doin' to my beautiful engine!" the engineer complained. "Call 'em off. For God's sake, I'll take you where you want to go, but don't let 'em mess up my engine like that!"

"Sir," Tyreen replied softly, "I appreciate what you are feeling. I respect a man who is true to his calling, and you, sir, have impressed me with that attribute. Please accept my apology for what must be done to your beautiful engine, and I hope that you understand that only the necessity of war would drive me to such a terrible desecration. I pray that one day you will forgive me."

Tyreen left the engineer and walked over to stand beside Chambers and Ferguson as they watched the men working over the train.

"What's the matter with the crybaby over there?" Chambers asked derisively.

"We're messing up his plaything," Ferguson said, and both men laughed.

"Major Chambers, Captain Ferguson," Tyreen said

coldly. "When I see men like the engineer and Mike Rindell on the side of the Yankees, and people like the two of you on our side, it causes me to question the correctness of our cause." He walked away from them and stood alone while the men continued to vandalize the engine.

By the time the men had finished with their job, the sun was quite low in the west, and Tyreen made the decision not to move until the next morning.

"Can we build fires, Colonel?" one of the men asked.

"Yes," Tyreen said. "But, sentries, I want you in the Yankee uniforms we took, so trade off the jackets when you are relieved."

"I guess that lets me out of guard duty," one of the soldiers quipped. At six feet six, he was the biggest of the group, and even the largest Yankee jacket would be too small for him.

"Don't you worry none, Dingus," another soldier said. "We'll give you two jackets, and you can walk two tours instead of one."

The bantering brought laughter, and as the men set about making their camp, Tyreen could not help but notice their high spirits. Then he saw Mrs. Mayhew sitting on a rock near one of the fires, staring morosely into the flames, and he walked over to join her.

"Good evening, Mrs. Mayhew," he said, propping his foot up on a large rock nearby. He rested his elbows on his knee. "Is there anything I can do to make you more comfortable?"

"Yes," she said sharply, wrapping her shawl around her more tightly. "You can let me go."

Tyreen shook his head and laughed softly. "I wish I could, ma'am. But the conditions of our little patrol are such that we may find it necessary to have a bargaining position."

"I see," she said. "So I am to be used as a thing of barter?"

"If necessary," Tyreen said.

"And if not necessary?"

"I'm sure we will be able to find some way to parole you back to your husband," Tyreen said.

"Colonel," she said, rising and turning to face Tyreen. "My husband is a very powerful man. You don't think for one moment he is merely going to sit by and—"

"Oh, I know Andy quite well," Tyreen interrupted. "He is a courageous and determined man. But he is also a sensible man. I don't think he will do anything rash."

Julia's green eyes showed her bewilderment. "You . . . you know my husband?"

Tyreen chuckled. "I was your husband's first commanding officer when he entered the service," he said. "Yes, ma'am. I know him. He's a good man." Tyreen paused for a long, pregnant moment, then added quietly, "A much better man, if I may say so, than Captain Ferguson."

Julia gasped and put her hand to her mouth. "Sir! Why do you feel compelled to make the comparison?"

"No particular reason," Tyreen replied. "I was just making an observation, that's all."

Julia bowed her head, and a moment later Tyreen saw tears rolling down her cheeks.

"Oh, Colonel Tyreen, will he ever forgive me?" she asked.

"There is nothing to forgive," Tyreen said.

"I'm afraid there is. You see . . ."

"There is nothing to forgive," Tyreen said resolutely. "Captain Ferguson is a turncoat, a cad, and a liar. No gentleman would believe anything he says, and though the exigencies of war have caused me to strain the boundaries of gentlemenly behavior, I still consider myself a member of that fraternity. And if I, with the questionable qualities of a gentleman, refuse to believe the lies of such a cad, then Andy Mayhew, who is truly one of the finest gentlemen I have ever known, will not even give such a foul rumor his ear."

"But shouldn't I tell him?" Julia asked. She

searched in her pocket for a moment and pulled out a hankie. "I feel so . . . so unclean in body and soul."

"And crushing your husband's spirit will cleanse you?" Tyreen asked.

Julia blotted her eyes and wiped her nose. "No, of course not. But—"

"No buts, my dear," Tyreen said, his outstretched hands patting her upper arms. "You will tell him nothing, and you will never speak of this to another living soul."

"But the burden of it . . ."

"Will be your penance," Tyreen said. He took one of her hands in his and squeezed it. "I'm afraid I can offer you nothing in the way of food but some jerky and a little coffee, which is made from parched corn. Nevertheless, it will make you feel better. I'll get it for you."

Tyreen started over toward the fire, where the coffee was being brewed.

"Colonel?" Julia called after him. He looked back toward her. "Thank you."

"Wait until you taste it before you thank me," he said.

"I didn't mean that."

"There's nothing else to thank me for. Remember?"

Julia smiled. "I remember," she said.

Thirty miles away, in Nashville, Mike Rindell and Leah Saunders were sitting down to supper in the restaurant of the Maxwell House Hotel. The Maxwell House was Nashville's newest hotel, built for the wealthy cotton merchants and visiting politicians who frequented Nashville before the war. Though still in civilian hands, it was now almost exclusively used by federal officers. Colonel MacAphee had secured two rooms in the hotel for Rindell and Leah. The soldiers who had been part of the original Gold Train guard detail were billeted in the barracks provided for the garrison soldiers in the city.

Because of its clientele, the dining room was hung

with a dozen regimental flags and banners. The officers who ate here took special pains to dress in their cleanest, most impressive uniforms. When Rindell and Leah entered the dining room, there was more than one whisper about the quartermaster officer who did not even bother to change from his field uniform.

"Probably had a difficult day issuing mess kits," Rindell heard one staff major say to his dinner companion.

For her part, Leah was no better prepared for dining in such an elegant setting. Though the other women were wearing what *Harper's Bazaar* called "evening toilettes," Leah was wearing what the same publication called a "mountain dress." Its cut and style allowed the wearer much more freedom of motion than the clothes women normally wore.

"I think our fellow diners would prefer that we eat outside," Leah said.

"Then they're going to have to throw us out," Rindell growled. "I haven't eaten or slept under a roof since I left Trailback."

"Trailback?"

"It's the plantation manor near Resaca where Colonel Tyreen has set up his headquarters," Rindell said.

"A plantation manor? Well, it would appear that life in the field does occasionaly have its compensations. And were there beautiful young Southern Belles to serve you?" Leah teased.

"Day and night," Rindell answered with a straight face.

The western sky was spread with glowing hues as the sun settled behind the hills west of Nashville. Vibrant bands of brilliant colors—gold, orange, red, magenta, and royal purple—put their beauty on display.

Mike Rindell stood in the window of his fifth-floor room and looked out over the city, all the way to its outer limits, where he could see the miles of entrenchments that completely encircled Nashville. The series of low-lying forts was connected by trench lines that were two rows deep. Inside the forts, officers and men lived in burrowlike dugouts called bombproofs. They had been built first by the Rebels to defend against Yankee invasion and, failing to do the job for the Confederates, had subsequently been strengthened and manned by Union troops to fight off a potential Rebel attack.

From Rindell's vantage point, the fortifications looked impregnable. The trenches were dotted with artillery positions every hundred yards and lined with sharpened stakes angled to slow an enemy attack. He could also see a hundred campfires as the troops on the defensive lines prepared for the night to come. Though the staff and garrison soldiers were billeted in barracks and confiscated hotels in the town, the soldiers on picket duty had it no easier than the troops in the field.

As Mike Rindell stood in the window, looking out over the environs of Nashville, he thought back over the day, a long and eventful one. He had failed to prevent the Gold Train from being taken, and he had failed in his mission to get it back.

Where is Tyreen? How did he get away from me? Rindell thought. The train could not have just disappeared into thin air.

When Rindell returned from his fruitless search down the Central Alabama track, the first thing he did was get medical attention for the men wounded in the clash with General Forrest. With that attended to, he then sent wires to all Union positions along both lines leading to the south, and even to the line leading back north, advising everyone to be on the lookout for the Gold Train. The stations on all three routes reported back that the train had not yet shown up. Using the authority of General Rosecrans, Rindell then advised them to put on additional guards to make certain that the train did not sneak through during the night.

Realistically, Rindell knew there was only one place the train could be. It had to have pulled off onto a siding somewhere. But once there, Tyreen had no choice but to wait. He could not abandon the train and go cross-country, because he had no transportation. The horses the raiders had ridden to South Tunnel had been scattered the moment Tyreen had taken over the train. That meant Tyreen had no mounts and no way to get back with the gold except by train.

"I know you're hiding out there, somewhere, Colonel," Rindell said quietly. "Waiting in the dark, trying to cook up some new little surprise for us. Well, you got away from me today, but you won't tomorrow. Tomorrow, my friend, I may have a few surprises of my own."

This had been a day full of surprises, and seeing Leah again was not the least of them. It had indeed been the most pleasant.

Rindell smiled, and for a moment he put the considerations of Colonel Tyreen and the quest for the Gold Train aside. Instead, he thought of Leah. They had taken their dinner together tonight and had a very pleasant time. He had almost forgotten how much he enjoyed her company. He thought back to the appointment he had broken with her in Baltimore. It had taken every ounce of self-control not to show up, but he felt that if he had gone that night, he might have lost control over his entire life.

Perhaps he had overreacted. But he knew there was something about her, some indefinable quality that threatened to take control of him. Rindell was not without experience with women, though he had let no woman become close to him. He knew the moment he met Leah Saunders, however, that she could do just that. It was not simply that she was pretty. He had known other women just as pretty, maybe even prettier. She was intelligent, but she was not the only intelligent woman he had ever known. She was independent, and he certainly admired that. No, there was much more to it than her being pretty, intelligent, and independent. What was it? Why could he not put his finger on it?

Rindell laughed. Maybe he was being done in by his nose. Tonight, at the dinner table, there had been a maddening fragrance to her . . . like a mixture of jasmine, honeysuckle, spicy carnation, and a hint of spearmint. This combined with an essence that was clearly her own, and he could swear it was still hanging in the air, even though she had not set foot in this room.

What a fascinating woman Leah Saunders was. She was like a little drop of morning dew. Seen from one angle, a dewdrop can turn a sunbeam into a brilliant burst of blue light. Tilt the head just so, and the dewdrop turns into a splash of crimson, a flash of gold, or any one of the colors of the rainbow.

Mike Rindell was acutely aware that he could, quite easily, fall in love with Leah Saunders. She was a danger to him—a beautiful, delightful danger, but a danger nevertheless. He would have to be on his guard to avoid falling into the tender trap that, however innocently, was being laid for him.

The next morning, Colonel Tyreen stood on a high rock precipice, looking out over a meadow whose wild mustard flowers and bachelor buttons created great swirls of yellow and blue. Behind him, his men were breaking camp, preparing for the run through Nashville and, if everything went well, on to Georgia.

Tyreen heard someone come up from his rear. There was a discreet cough.

"Colonel, we're ready."

Tyreen looked around. It was Bryant Clark, his newly appointed sergeant. With Sergeant Booker a prisoner of war of the Yankees and Captain Rindell a Yankee agent, Tyreen had felt a tremendous loneliness envelope him. He had no sense of rapport with Blackie Chambers, and he found Captain Ferguson just as dislikable. Clark, the young man who had advised him about the necessity of grease for the wheel bearings and debeautifying the engine, had been thrust into that gap. Tyreen had promoted him to sergeant as a reward for those contributions, but also as a means of elevating one of the men to a position of rank that would allow him to have someone to communicate with, though Clark did not realize it.

"Thank you, Sergeant Clark," Tyreen said. He had been drinking the parched-corn coffee that was serving much of the South during this time of travail, and he swallowed the rest, then put his cup in his haversack. "Let's get aboard. Oh, and Sergeant?"

"Yes, sir."

"You ride in the car with Mrs. Mayhew. Make her as comfortable as you can, under the circumstances, would you?"

"Yes, sir. Colonel, you know . . ." Clark started. Then he stopped, letting the sentence hang in the air.

"Yes?"

"It's Mrs. Mayhew. She seems different this morning. I don't know what it is . . . she ain't complainin' as much, and she's bein' . . . well, almost nice."

Tyreen smiled. "Put yourself in her position, Sergeant Clark. Under the circumstances, I would say she has shown remarkable restraint."

"Yes, sir," Clark said.

When Tyreen returned to the train, he saw the engineer standing alongside the track, looking up at the engine. When it had left Washington four days ago, it had been the pride of the U.S. Military Railroad; now it looked as if it had been subjected to rough treatment and no care. It was scarred, spotted, and splashed with grease and dirt.

"Mr. Engineer, it's time to go," Tyreen said gently.

"Colonel, it's more than just messin' up the engine. I mean look at the filth. Who would be caught dead in such a machine?"

"I'm sorry," Tyreen said.

The engineer gave a sigh, then climbed into the cab,

with Tyreen mounting right behind him. The fireman was already on board and had stoked the fire until the steam pressure was up. Chambers and Ferguson were leaning out the window on the opposite side, laughing over some joke.

"Good morning, gentlemen," Tyreen greeted them.

"Colonel," Chambers said as he turned around. Ferguson just nodded.

Tyreen noticed then that the gold had been moved and was now stacked on the floor of the locomotive itself. "What's this doing up here?" he asked.

"It was Ferguson's idea," Chambers explained.

"Colonel, we lost one car yesterday," Ferguson said as he stepped away from the window. "Suppose we had to lose another, then another, and then another? Why, if we have the gold right up here with us, it won't make any difference how many cars we lose. As long as the engine is still going, we still have the gold."

"Yes, sir," Chambers added. "And as bad as those cars are, they may just break free on their own."

Colonel Tyreen stroked his whiskers with his hook. He hated admitting it, but what Chambers and Ferguson said made sense. "All right," he agreed. "Now, then, Mr. Engineer, let's get this train under way."

The engineer opened the throttle, and the train began to roll. Before they had gone a hundred yards, the engineer yelled above the sound of the engine, "I don't know whether we're gonna make it or not. Can't you feel that?"

"Feel what?"

"The flat wheels on all them cars."

Actually, Tyreen felt nothing, but when he leaned out the window and looked back along the string of rusty freight cars, he could hear that they were much louder than the passenger cars had been. He could also see that they were riding rougher. At least none of the wheels were smoking; the grease and Sergeant Clark had taken care of that. He pulled back in through the window and looked at the engineer.

"Just keep it slow and steady," he said.

"Yes, sir," the engineer replied.

The train continued on for another half hour, not traveling much faster than a man could run, though some progress was clearly being made. As they drew close enough to Nashville to see the city in the distance, Captain Ferguson suddenly drew his pistol and faced the others in the engine cab.

"Colonel, would you hand me your pistol, please?" Ferguson asked.

"What?" Tyreen replied, surprised by the sudden and unexpected action.

"Your pistol, please," Ferguson said again.

Tyreen looked around at the other men in the cab. The fireman and engineer appeared to be just as shocked by Ferguson's action. Chambers just stood there, looking on.

"You," Ferguson said to the fireman. "Pull the colonel's pistol out slowly, using just two fingers."

The fireman reached over and pulled out Tyreen's gun, then handed it to Ferguson.

"What is this?" Tyreen said. "A *double* double cross? Are you working for the Yankees after all?"

"Not exactly," Ferguson said. He smiled broadly. "I've gone into business for myself."

"Meaning you want the gold."

"A brilliant observation, Colonel."

Tyreen sighed. "For a moment there, I was about to regain some respect for you. I thought maybe you had a sense of duty after all. I see that I was mistaken."

"You were mistaken, Colonel. But you don't have to be a fool."

"What do you mean?"

"Why, I mean you can join Blackie and me in this little venture."

"Blackie?" Tyreen asked in surprise. He looked at his second in command and saw that Major Chambers had now pulled his own pistol and was standing beside Ferguson. "So, you are in this, too? You must have had a busy night, convincing him to go along with you."

Both Ferguson and Chambers laughed out loud.

"Did I say something funny?"

"Yes," Chambers said. "Do you really think this is just something we came up with last night?"

"You mean you didn't?"

"Oh, no, Colonel. This is something Gerald and I have had in mind for a long time. Since way before you even knew about the gold. You will recall, won't you, that I was the one who brought you the news of the shipment?"

"Yes, I recall," Tyreen said softly. He was outraged that yet another of his officers had turned against him—and against their cause.

"I knew Gerald and I couldn't pull it off alone," Chambers continued. "But with Tyreen's Raiders it would be a cinch."

"I see."

"You can join us, Colonel," Ferguson offered. "One million dollars in gold is enough money for all three of us."

"And just what do you propose to do with it?" Tyreen asked.

"Well, sir, to begin with, we aren't going to take the Nashville and Georgia line; we're going to take the Central Alabama. You see, my cousin is an officer on General Nathan Bedford Forrest's staff, and I've arranged for him to persuade the general to move up along the Central Alabama line, taking control as far north as he can. That way, we'll get into Southern territory very fast."

"And once you're in Southern territory?"

"Why, it's simple," Ferguson said, smiling broadly. "We'll go all the way to Mobile. We've arranged for a boat to meet us there and help us run the blockade. After that, we'll land somewhere up north, where we can live out our lives as wealthy gentlemen."

"Wealthy, perhaps," Tyreen said. He shook his head. "But you'll never be gentlemen. You'll never be anything but scoundrels!"

"I'm sorry you feel that way, Colonel," Ferguson

said. "As you can see, we have made every plan. If you would throw in with us, it would go smoother. The risks are greater without you, but so are the rewards. It really makes no difference to me. So, what is your decision?"

"I gave you my decision, you treasonous bastards!" Tyreen said.

"Too bad," Ferguson said. Without blinking an eye, he pulled the trigger.

There was a flash of light and a loud pop as his gun discharged. Tyreen felt the burn of a slug in his stomach. It hit him with the impact of a kicking mule, knocking him across the engine platform. He reached up with his hook in a futile attempt to grab for the mounting assist rail, missed, then felt himself tumble out of the train. He landed on his back on the rock ballast of the railroad bed, then slid, head first, down the embankment into the ditch that ran parallel to the railroad.

Up above he could hear the bump and rattle of the flat-wheeled cars as the train passed him. He saw Sergeant Clark standing in the doorway of the first car, but Clark was not looking down and did not see him. He opened his mouth to yell, but no sound came out. A moment later, the train had completely passed him, and when he raised his head, he saw the last car, receding rapidly. Then he passed out.

Back on board the engine, Blackie Chambers climbed out onto the mounting step and, holding onto the assist rail, leaned way out to look back along the length of the train to where Tyreen had fallen.

"Do you see him?" Ferguson yelled down to him.

"He's not moving," Chambers called back.

"Good. The son of a bitch is probably dead," Ferguson replied.

Chambers started to climb back into the train. That was when he saw the fireman, his shovel raised, coming up behind Ferguson, who for the moment had his back to the cab crew.

"Look out!" Chambers shouted, and Ferguson turned around quickly, firing his pistol almost in the same action. His bullet caught the fireman in the throat, and he dropped his shovel, gagged, and put his hand over the wound. He fell back against the stacked boxes of gold, then lay there with his eyes open and unseeing, already dead.

"Charlie!" the engineer yelled, going to his friend.

By now Chambers had reentered the cab.

"You bastard!" the engineer hissed. "You killed Charlie!"

"I didn't have any choice," Ferguson said. "The son of a bitch came after me with a shovel. Come on, Blackie, help me push him off. Then you and I are going to have to take turns keeping the engine fired."

"Maybe not," Chambers said. "I'll go back and get one of the men. They loved that old bastard Tyreen. If they think he and the fireman killed each other, they'll rally behind us when I tell them Tyreen would expect them to do their duty."

"What about the engineer?" Ferguson asked. "What if he tells the man you bring up here what really happened?"

"Then we'll kill him—and the man he tells," Chambers replied matter-of-factly.

Chapter 11

THE HOTEL RESTAURANT HAD NOT YET OPENED ITS DOORS for breakfast that morning when Mike Rindell left the hotel and walked down Church Street to the railroad yard. At this hour Nashville could have been any town, anywhere. The aroma of biscuits in the oven and bacon in the pan wafted onto the street from scores of houses. Here, a baby cried; there, a little girl laughed. It was hard to believe that the entire city had been turned into an advanced outpost for an army at war.

But then Rindell walked past the Taylor Depot, the largest military warehouse in the world, and all that changed.

Inside the open doors, Rindell saw hundreds of soldiers stacking blankets, shoes, tents, and other equipment. He thought of his own six months with the Confederate Army, and the privations they were suffering. When Colonel MacAphee had given him his commission in the Union's Quartermaster Corps yesterday, he had told him about some of what was contained in these buildings.

"There's fifteen million rations," MacAphee had bragged, "two-hundred thousand blankets, four-hundred-fifty thousand pair of shoes, half a million tents, half a million great coats, and twenty million rounds of ammunition."

The figures had been impressive. Mike Rindell thought that if everyone in authority in the Confederacy could visit this place, they would see at once the futility of continuing the war. This was just one Union supply depot, but more equipment was contained in this row of unpainted, slab-sided buildings than the entire Army of the Confederacy had seen in the last two years.

As Rindell walked along one of the tracks that passed the depot, a flatcar caught his attention. At one end of the car he saw a large box. At the other end, a wicker basket, obviously a balloon basket, and a huge pile of silk in various colors. The box he recognized from the balloon ascension he had seen in Washington. It was a hydrogen generator. He knew how the generator worked. By passing steam over hot iron in a tube, it would isolate the hydrogen content of the water. A generator of this sort would be able to inflate a balloon within an hour.

"It's the Silkdress Balloon," MacAphee said when Rindell asked him about it later in the colonel's office. "You may have heard of it."

"Yes," Rindell said. "Yes, I did hear of it. Ladies from all over the South donated their ball gowns and party dresses to supply the material for the balloon envelope. But what is it doing here?"

"It hasn't made an ascension since the summer of sixty-two," MacAphee explained. "The Rebels brought it up here during their defense of Nashville. Unfortunately for them, a strong gust of wind snatched it from the ground and deposited it in our territory. We've had it ever since."

"Has it been aloft?"

"Heavens, no!" MacAphee said. "We don't have any aeronauts here."

Mike Rindell leaned forward in his seat and said with a grin, "I'm going to take it up. With your permission, of course."

The colonel was clearly shocked, but it was not the first time the young Faraday agent had had that effect on MacAphee. "You? Are you a qualified balloonist?"

"What's there to being qualified?" Rindell asked. "You fill the bag with gas, stand in the gondola, and hold on. When the balloon goes up, you go up. That's all there is to it."

"I don't know," MacAphee said. "I'd hate to think—"

"Colonel MacAphee," Rindell said with a frustrated sigh, "it's the only chance I have of finding the Gold Train. I'm convinced they've pulled off onto a siding somewhere, intending to wait us out. Now if I can go aloft and have a look around, I might be able to spot them."

MacAphee studied Rindell for a long moment, then shrugged. "All right," he said. "But you'd better let me clear it with General Rosecrans so a message can be sent out to our lines. Otherwise, you might get shot down by our own people."

"Get the message out in a hurry then," Rindell instructed. "I'm going to move the balloon out into an open area and begin an immediate inflation."

MacAphee smiled broadly. "You know, I'm looking forward to this. It's been quite a while since we had a balloon ascension around here. It'll be good for the men's morale."

The excitement spread quickly, and Mike Rindell had no trouble finding volunteers to operate the generator and play out the lines for him. Nearly a hundred people were gathered around the flatcar as the inflation process began. As they stood watching, a freight train entered the yard.

"Make way, there!" one of the soldiers yelled, and several of them had to clear the tracks for a slow-moving train.

"Whooeee, will you look at that train? I ain't never seen cars in as bad a shape or a locomotive as dirty as that," another said.

"Looks like it's been rode hard and put away wet," a third soldier suggested, and the men laughed at the observation.

Inside that same slow-moving locomotive, Gerald Ferguson glanced through the window at the crowd of men who were gathered around the flatcar.

"What's going on?" Blackie Chambers asked. Chambers, who was still wearing a Confederate uniform, was sitting on the fireman's bench, out of sight, so as not to be noticed by anyone in the track yard.

"I don't know," Ferguson answered. "A lot of men gathered around a railroad car for some reason. Looks like something on the car . . . a pile of old clothing perhaps."

"Probably dividing up the booty they looted from the homes of the South," Chambers said.

"Here, now, my Southern friend," Ferguson teased. "Would you deny such enterprise from my comrades in arms? Especially considering what you and I are doing?"

Chambers laughed. "The only thing I got against 'em is they don't think big enough," he said.

"You bastards think you're pretty smart, don't you?" the engineer spat.

"As smart as we need to be," Ferguson said. "Just see that you are smart. Keep your hands away from that whistle cord. You do anything that I think is a signal . . . or anything that even makes me nervous, and I'll shoot you."

"Who'll drive your train then?" the engineer asked.

"I've been watching; I can do it. You push that lever one way and it goes, bring it back and it stops."

"There's a lot more to it than that."

"I'll take my chances on the rest," Ferguson said.

"Hold it!" Chambers suddenly said, standing up

and looking through the window. "That switch just ahead. That's where we pick up the Central Alabama track."

"I'll run ahead and move it," Ferguson volunteered. "You keep an eye on our friend."

Ferguson jumped down from the creeping engine, then ran ahead of it and turned the handle that moved the twin rails into the proper position. The truck wheels caught the new track, then the drivers, then the entire train began curving off that track and onto the other.

Though a normal switchman would have reset the track after the entire train had passed over it, Ferguson left the lever as it was. Sprinting back down the track, he finally caught up with the engine. Reaching up to grab the assist rail, he jumped onto the step, hung on for a moment, then climbed back into the cab.

"All right, Mr. Engineer," Chambers said. "You may increase your speed. We're heading south!"

"Don't call me Mr. Engineer. The name's Harris."

"Colonel Tyreen called you Mr. Engineer."

Harris scowled at Chambers. "Colonel Tyreen was a gentleman. He knew how to use the term with respect. You don't."

"Very well, Mr. Harris," Chambers said, twisting his mouth on the name. "You may increase your speed."

"If I go much over twenty miles per hour, I'll break the string of cars," Harris warned. "Flat wheels like that put a lot of strain on the couplers."

"We'll just have to take that chance."

"Beware the line, sir!" a soldier shouted, and the officer who had been cautioned had to step lively to avoid getting his leg entangled in one of the many ropes dangling from the balloon.

The Silkdress Balloon, though not sufficiently filled to be bouyant, was now fully shaped by the gas and was moments away from being able to lift off. The work had been quick and expert, since one of the soldiers disclosed that he had been with Thaddeus Lowe during the professor's ascensions for General McClellan during the Peninsular campaigns.

"When I'm ready, cast off all lines but one," Rindell instructed them. "Don't let that line go, or I shall be at the whim of the elements."

"We'll hang on to it, Captain," his balloon expert told him.

"Good, good. I'm counting on you."

"Good morning, Mike," a woman's voice called, and Rindell looked around to see that Leah Saunders was just arriving on the site. She looked at the balloon and the preparations for its launching. "I see you've been busy this morning."

"Yes," Rindell answered, smiling broadly. He pointed at the balloon. "Not exactly Ezekiel's chariot, but I think it'll get the job done."

"I agree. We should be able to see for miles when we are aloft."

"We? What do you mean, we?" Rindell asked, his eyes narrowing with suspicion.

"Well, you didn't think for one moment I was going to let you go up while I stay down here, did you?" Leah answered coquettishly. "Besides, an extra pair of hands is often necessary when handling the ballast and valve rope."

"Valve rope? Ballast?"

"To say nothing of the rip panel rope," Leah said matter-of-factly.

"Leah, do you understand balloons?"

She smiled, then walked over to the balloon and began pointing to the various components. "This is the suspension hoop," she said. "This the drag rope. These are the suspension ropes, and this, the netting. That's the inlet valve, and there, on the side of the envelope, is the rip panel. That is for discharging gas rapidly."

"Where did you learn about all this?"

"I've made quite a few ascensions," Leah said. "My

uncle thought ballooning was a great sporting adventure. He built one."

Rindell stepped toward the basket and held his hand out in a gesture of invitation. "Then, by all means, be my guest on this ascension. In fact, it might be better if you would busy yourself with the necessary aeronautical functions, while I act as an observer."

"Why, Captain Rindell, how nice of you to invite me," Leah teased.

"Captain, the balloon's ready anytime you are," the veteran of Lowe's balloon corps announced.

"Then I suppose we are ready, too," Rindell answered. He helped Leah get into the basket, then climbed in beside her.

"All right, Sergeant," Leah said, nodding as she took her position. "Please release all the lines except for the tether line, which you need to play out slowly as we rise."

"You," the sergeant called to the men at the windlass. "Play the line out as the balloon ascends. The rest of you . . . away all lines!"

The lines fell away, and Leah tossed over a couple of bags of ballast as the tether line went slack, and then she indicated that Rindell should do the same. He did so, and the balloon began rising straight up, since there was almost no discernable breeze.

As long as Mike Rindell was looking toward the distant horizon, he had no particular illusion of height. A moment later, however, he happened to look straight down over the edge of the basket. When he did, he saw that the men who had been a part of the launch process, but moments before, were now exceptionally foreshortened by the angle and altitude the balloon had reached.

Leah tossed over another couple of bags of ballast, as did Rindell, and the rate of ascension increased.

Now the balloon was high enough that he could quite easily see all the way to the edge of the city, to the same fortifications he had observed from the window of his hotel room last night. From this vantage point, however, he could quite clearly see the intricate filigree formed by the lines as they angled this way and that, forming a neat, geometric pattern around the entire perimeter of the city.

To the north Rindell could see the bow of the Cumberland river; to the south, the fields and hills, though by now the hills were but small ridges that did nothing to obscure his vision. And from here, Rindell could see all the railroads coming into and going out of Nashville.

On the other side of the Cumberland to the north, he saw a fast passenger train approaching the city. To the south, on the Central Alabama line, a very slow freight chugged its way toward Franklin. The Nashville and Georgia road and the Kingston Spur were both empty.

"Be sure to look on all the sidings," Rindell said, handing a pair of field glasses to Leah. Taking the other pair, he swept the horizon for as far as he could see, from this altitude a considerable distance.

"There's something on a siding over there," Leah said, pointing from her side of the car.

"You're pointing to the west. He wouldn't have gone that way. That's the Kingston Spur."

Leah lowered the glasses and looked at Rindell. "Yes, but if he was going to hide out, wouldn't that be the place you'd least expect him?"

Rindell paused. "Maybe so. But what good would it do him? He'd have to come right back through the yard to escape, and we'd surely see him."

"You're probably right," Leah said, again raising the glasses to her eyes. "I don't see any locomotive with it, anyway. I guess . . . Mike!" she suddenly gasped.

"What is it?"

"That second car on the siding . . . That's the kitchen car from our train!"

Rindell looked through the glasses and saw that three passenger cars, a kitchen car, and a baggage car were sitting on the siding.

"Are you sure that's the same car?"

"Positive," she said.

"How do we get back down?"

"This way," Leah said, pulling on the rip panel to vent the gas. The balloon began descending very quickly, and less than a minute later they were crawling out of the basket to the applause of the gathered soldiers who had treated the ascent as a show.

"What did you see?" MacAphee asked when they returned to the supply station.

"We saw the cars from the train," Rindell said as he climbed out of the basket. "They're sitting on a siding to the west, off the Kingston Spur."

"No locomotive?"

"No," Rindell said, helping Leah out. "But it has to be somewhere out there. My guess is they've found another siding to hide the engine on. I'm going to take the *Union* and have a look at the cars to make sure the gold isn't on them. The siding can't be more than ten miles from here, and the engine could well be just beyond it."

Leah and Rindell accompanied the colonel back to his office. As Rindell made preparations for the run along the track toward the cars they had seen, Leah began studying the schedule for freight and passenger trains.

"Colonel MacAphee," she called. "I see here that the passenger train we saw coming toward Nashville from the north is on your schedule."

"Yes," MacAphee said. "You probably saw the nine-oh-five."

"But we also saw a freight, heading south on the Central Alabama line. I don't see a schedule for it."

"Yes, I saw it leaving the yard a short time ago," MacAphee said. "If you noticed, it definitely was not a

U.S.M.R. train. Since we've retaken Tennessee, we've allowed some of the civilian freight companies to resume operation. All we require from them is that their schedule not interfere with ours. Otherwise, we don't keep track of when they come or when they go."

A short whistle outside the depot let them know that the *Union* was ready again. Rindell and Leah climbed aboard, and a moment later they were pounding out of the station, moving as swiftly as they had the night before.

"Major?" the engineer said from where he sat in the cab of the Gold Train. "You see that signal ahead?"

"What about it?" Blackie Chambers asked. He was leaning against the back wall of the cab, chewing on a toothpick.

"It's a blocking signal," Harris explained. "We can't go any farther than that."

"The hell you say. Run through it," Chambers ordered.

The engineer turned around and looked at the major. "We can't. That's an order to stop. I can't ignore it."

"What if you do?"

"They can change the track so that we got no choice. We got to stop."

Blackie Chambers rubbed his chin thoughtfully and looked over at Gerald Ferguson, who was sitting on a stool near a window. "You have any suggestions?" he asked.

Ferguson looked at the engineer. Putting his feet up on another stool and leaning against the wall, he locked his hands behind his head and said, "Harris, you look like what they call a God-fearing man. Would that be true?"

"I don't find it necessary to boast of the fact, but yes, I count myself as one of the Lord's sheep."

"Then as a God-fearing man, Harris, you would do everything you could to keep harm from coming to an innocent person, wouldn't you? Especially if that person was a woman . . . say the wife of a general and the niece of the secretary of treasury?"

"What . . . what have you got in mind?" Harris asked.

"I'm going back into the car where Mrs. Mayhew is being held prisoner," Ferguson explained. "And I'm going to kill her."

"What?" Harris gasped.

"You heard me," Ferguson said. "I'm going to kill her. That is, unless you find some way to talk us through this block signal."

"Captain, you don't just find some way," Harris protested. "A block signal is a block signal, and it has to be obeyed."

"So do my orders," Ferguson said coldly. "We'd better be moving again, and moving very quickly, or the woman dies."

Ferguson let his feet drop to the floor of the cab. He stood up, walked to the rear of the compartment, and climbed up on the tender. But before he left, he looked back at the engineer. "I'll be watching you, every moment," he said.

"I—I'll do what I can to get us through," Harris agreed. The man's face had grown noticeably ashen.

As the freight moved slowly into the depot, Harris pulled on the brake. Then, setting the throttle bar to vent the excess steam, he climbed down the side of the engine and walked over to talk to the stationmaster.

Inside the first boxcar Gerald Ferguson stood with Julia Mayhew. His left arm gripped her roughly, while his left hand clamped tightly against her mouth. In his right he held a pistol, pointed at her temple.

"You make one sound to cause him to look in here, and I'll blow your brains all over the inside of this car," he hissed.

Julia could scarcely believe this man who so terrorized her now was the same man with whom she had once shared her bed.

In the other cars Tyreen's Raiders, unaware that they were no longer part of a patriotic mission but were now the pawns of a criminal conspiracy, stayed quiet. They knew they could overpower the stationmaster and probably anyone he had with him. But they also knew the wheels were so flat that an ordinary horse could easily outrun them. They would not be able to get too far once word was out as to who they were. Their best bet continued to be secrecy.

The soldiers strained to hear the conversation between the engineer and the stationmaster.

"What is it?" Harris asked as he walked toward the stationmaster, pointing to the block. "I see we can't go through."

"We got orders from Nashville," the stationmaster said. "We're to search all the trains before we let them through."

"Search them? Search them for what?"

"Gold," the stationmaster said. "Seems there was a special government train carrying gold and a general's wife, but the whole train got stole by the Rebs."

Harris looked back at his train, at the rusting cars, the dirty engine. He forced a laugh.

"You think a general's wife would ride on something like this?"

"I figure she's probably ridin' in that first car there," the stationmaster said.

Ferguson cocked his pistol, and there was a collective holding of breath.

Suddenly the stationmaster laughed out loud. "Yes, sir," he said, "I figure you got her a throne made out of hay bales. And the gold? Why, most likely, all them cars is full of it!" He laughed again.

Harris laughed with him.

The stationmaster walked over to the switch and moved it, taking off the blocking signal. Still laughing, he motioned them through.

"You go on through, now," he said. "And you give

my regards to the general's wife. Tell her I hope she's real comfortable in that parlor car you got fixed up for her." With the signal moved, the stationmaster returned to his office to share with the others the joke of a general's wife being transported in a train that looked like this one.

Harris climbed back into the engine cab and moved the throttle bar, not looking at Ferguson and Chambers. Slowly, very slowly, the train began to creep forward.

"You did very well," Chambers said in a low voice as the train got under way.

"If it hadn't been for the lady," Harris muttered, "I would've told him just what and who was in this train."

"And been killed for your troubles," Chambers reminded him.

"Mister, there's some things that're worth dyin' for," Harris said. "And seein' you get yours would be one of them."

On board the *Union*, about five miles west of Nashville on the Kingston Spur, Mike Rindell was squinting as he searched the horizon before him for some sign of the abandoned cars. But his attention was diverted when suddenly he saw someone rise up from the side of the track in front of him. The apparition held up both arms, and Rindell saw at once that it had one hand and one hook.

"My God!" he gasped. "It's Tyreen! Engineer, back this thing down!"

The engineer threw on the emergency brake and, when the wheels were locked, moved the Johnson lever to throw them into reverse. A shower of sparks spewed forth from the great driver wheels, which were now spinning in the opposite direction of travel. Despite the reverse action of the wheels, the high speed at which they had been traveling, as well as the great mass of the train, caused them to continue to slide forward for several hundred feet more. Finally the train stopped, and Rindell jumped out and ran back along the track until he reached Tyreen.

Colonel Jebediah Tyreen was standing alongside the track, holding himself up by leaning against a telegraph pole. When Rindell approached him, Tyreen greeted him with a wan smile.

"Hello, Mike," the colonel said. His face was ashen, and Rindell saw that the front of his tunic and top of his pants were covered with blood. He was holding his hand over his wound, and his hand and the sleeve of his jacket were also red. "What are you doing out here?"

"Colonel Tyreen. What happened?"

"Blackie Chambers," Tyreen said. "He and that traitor Ferguson shot me."

The exertion Tyreen had expended finally took its toll, and he passed out. Rindell rushed to him, calling for help from a couple of his men. Together they lifted the unconscious colonel and carried him to the car the *Union* was pulling. After laying him on the wooden floor, one of the soldiers removed his jacket, folding it for use as a pillow.

"Colonel? Colonel, what happened?" Mike Rindell asked gently when the older man showed signs of consciousness a minute later. "Why did they shoot you?"

"Did . . . did you catch him?" Tyreen asked, his voice weak. "Did you get the bastard?"

"No, sir, not yet. We figure he's out here, though, hiding his engine on one of these sidings. And much as it pains me to admit it, that makes for a pretty slick operation."

"No," Tyreen said, shaking his head. The word came out in a long hiss, and Rindell knew that Tyreen was in a great deal of pain. "He's not here. He stole the gold, Mike."

"Yes, well, all of you stole the gold."

"No. I mean Chambers stole the gold from us. He and Ferguson, they've taken it all. They don't give a damn about the Confederacy." The colonel's face twisted with pain. "They plan to go all the way to Mobile, then steal a boat and get away."

"Well, I'll be damned," Rindell said. "So patriotism and loyalty had nothing to do with it after all. They just used us . . . both of us . . . to get what they wanted. Well, we'll get him."

"The train's not out here. He took it away."

Mike Rindell frowned. "How? We saw every train in the yard that moved."

"Change . . . change . . ." Tyreen said, his head rolling from side to side. He passed out before he could finish what he was trying to say.

One of the men traveling with Rindell was a medical clerk. He had begun examining Tyreen the moment they had laid him on the floor of the car. When Tyreen passed out this time, the clerk looked at Rindell and said, "Captain, we've got to get him back to the hospital right away."

"All right," Rindell agreed. "We might as well go back to Nashville anyway. Tyreen said Chambers and Ferguson weren't up here, and I believe him. I'll tell the engineer to get us back as quickly as he can."

With Tyreen made as comfortable as possible, the train scooted back into the train yard in just a little over five minutes. Tyreen was taken off the train and hurried to the hospital, just one block away from the depot. Mike Rindell and Leah Saunders went with him.

"He's been hurt bad, Doctor," Rindell told the surgeon. "Can you save him? Can you get the bullet out?"

The doctor pushed opened Tyreen's eyelids and looked into his eyes, then shook his head.

"There's nothing we can do for him," he said. "He's dying."

Rindell sent one of the men who had helped transport the colonel back to the depot for Sergeant Booker and Private Ebenezer Scruggs, authorizing their release to his custody. They arrived twenty minutes later, hurrying over to the side of their dying commander.

"Cap'n, I wanna thank you for lettin' me an' Ebenezer come see him," Booker said to Rindell.

"He's in an enemy camp," Rindell said. "I wanted him to have some friends around him. I'm afraid I forfeited the right to be counted among that number."

Unexpectedly, Tyreen opened his eyes. "I still consider you my friend," he said, surprising Rindell. The colonel looked around. "Booker, Ebenezer, I'm glad to see you two are all right."

"Yes, sir. We're fine," Booker said quietly.

Tyreen saw Leah standing beside Rindell.

"You'll pardon me, ma'am, for not rising in the presence of a lady," he said, a faint smile on his lips.

"Of course, Colonel," Leah replied.

"Booker, Scruggs . . . don't let Chambers get away with it," Tyreen said, his voice becoming more a whisper. "I want you two to help the captain and this young lady. Help them get the gold back."

Booker's brows knitted together. "Colonel, you don't mean help the Yankees?"

"Yes, I do mean it. Don't you see, Booker? Chambers and Ferguson have taken the gold for their own use. If it can't be used by the Confederacy, I'll be damned if I'll let those scoundrels have it. I'd rather see it back in the hands of the Yankees."

"But, Colonel, you said yourself you would hang Cap'n Rindell if you were given the chance," Booker reminded him.

"Hang him for a spy, yes, but not for a traitor. Captain Rindell might be for the other side, Sergeant Booker, but he is a man of honest convictions and, therefore, a man of honor." Tyreen suddenly broke into a spasm of coughing, and by the time it was over, his entire face was covered with sweat.

Booker, because he could do nothing else to comfort his colonel, began wiping his brow. "All right, Colonel. I'll help him," he said.

The colonel's glassy eyes turned toward the private. "And you, Scruggs?"

"Me, too," Ebenezer put in.

Tyreen forced himself to rise up on his elbows. "Raise your right hands, both of you. Do you swear an oath not to fight against the United States again?"

Booker and Scruggs looked at each other in confusion for a moment, but then both of them raised their hands.

"Yes, sir. We swear that," Booker said, nodding.

"Private Scruggs, it has to come from your own lips."

"Yes, sir," Ebenezer said. "I swear it."

Tyreen let out a long sigh, then lay back down on the pillow. "That's a solemn oath, administered to you by an officer. You can't go back on it."

"No, sir, we won't," Booker promised.

"Captain Rindell, you heard their oath. I want you to grant them a parole so they can help you."

"All right," Rindell said.

"Good." Jebediah Tyreen closed his eyes for a moment. "Now, men, go get Chambers and Ferguson."

"Colonel," Rindell said, "if Chambers and Ferguson aren't hiding on some siding up Kingston Spur, where are they?"

Tyreen coughed again, and this time the spasms were so great that he began bleeding again. Alarmed, Leah called for the doctor, and he came quickly to Tyreen's bedside.

"You'd better leave now," the doctor said. "He's dying. I'm going to knock him out with laudanum so that he can stand the pain."

"Wait," Tyreen gasped. "I . . . I have to tell . . . *Change* . . . change train."

"Changed trains? Damn, you mean they stole another train?"

"Change," Tyreen gasped. He nodded his head desperately and tried again. "Change."

Tyreen drew just two more breaths before he let his last breath out in a long, life-surrendering death rattle. Then the breathing stopped. The doctor felt his pulse. It fluttered once, then was still. He pulled the sheet over the Rebel colonel's head.

"Cap'n?" Booker asked. "Did you mean what you told the colonel 'bout lettin' us help you find the bastards that did this?"

"If you meant your oath, I meant it," Rindell said.

Booker and Ebenezer looked at each other for a moment, and then both nodded.

"We meant it," Booker said.

Rindell smiled. "It'll be good to have you two men on my side again," he said.

When Rindell, Leah, Booker, and Ebenezer left the hospital, they were met by a sergeant, who saluted and said, "Captain Rindell, the patrol is back."

Rindell had sent a patrol racing down the Kingston Spur, just to make certain that the gold had not for some reason been left on the abandoned cars.

"Did they find anything?" he asked.

"Neither hide nor hair of the gold or of Ferguson," the sergeant reported. "But we found a dead man alongside the track. One of the fellers was with the original guard detail that brought the gold out here. He said the man we found was the fireman on the Gold Train."

"That makes two men they've murdered. . . ."

"Plus Sarah Cunningham," Leah added.

"Then I plan to stop him. I just wish I knew what other train he took."

"Mike? What about the freight we saw?"

"The freight? I doubt it, if he was going to steal another train, he wouldn't . . ." Rindell started. Then he paused and flashed a triumphant smile at Leah. "Change train!" he suddenly said.

"What?" Leah asked.

"Leah, they didn't change trains! They changed the

train they had! They disguised the Gold Train. They took down the diamond stack, they dropped the passenger cars and took on freight cars. Damn! We let them slip by, right under our noses."

"Maybe so," Leah said. She smiled broadly at Rindell. "But they won't slip by again."

Chapter 12

ONCE MORE, THE *UNION* WAS PRESSED INTO SERVICE. Rindell, Leah, Booker, Ebenezer, and the little contingent of soldiers—who were now calling themselves Rindell's Rail Warriors—started out in pursuit of the freight train Rindell and Leah had seen heading south. This time, however, the *Union* was pulling one extra car. Mike Rindell had ordered the flatcar with the gas generator and partially deflated balloon to be connected to the train.

Just before they left, Rindell and the others heard the welcome news that General Forrest had been driven south of Pulaski. Rindell realized, however, that the Gold Train had such a lead that even at the slow rate it was traveling, it would still be behind Rebel lines before he could catch up to it.

The *Union* thundered south, creating quite a stir as it did. In addition to the interest it normally generated, the added attraction of a balloon partially rising above the last car drew even more spectators. Then, just below Pulaski, someone ran onto the tracks in front of the train, waving his arms in a desperate attempt to stop them. The engineer threw on the brakes, and the train skidded for several feet, the shrieking sound of metal sliding on metal drowning out all other sound.

The engine was no sooner stopped than Rindell saw the reason they had been flagged down. A rail had been taken up in front of them. Had they continued, the train would have tipped over, and at the speed they were traveling several would have been killed.

"I'm a Confederate," the farmer who stopped them said. "But I don't hold with deliberately wreckin' a train and killin' folks. So when I seen what them folks on the other train done, I figured to wait right here and flag down the next train to come along, no matter whether it be Yank or Reb."

"Thanks, mister," Leah said. "You saved our lives."

"I guess I particular wouldn't have wanted to see a woman get kilt this way," the farmer said.

"Let's go!" Mike Rindell shouted to the soldiers with him. "We've got to get the rail back in place!"

A dozen soldiers jumped down from the train and hurried over to pick up the rail. Then they saw that in addition to being taken up, the rail had been bent before being dropped into the ditch alongside the track. It would be impossible to use it.

"We could send a wire to Nashville and ask them to bring us another rail," the engineer suggested. "Though it'll more'n likely take them the better part of an hour to get it to us."

"Cap'n," Booker said. "If you don't mind takin' a suggestion from an ex-Rebel, I got an idea."

"All right, let's hear it."

"Go ahead an' send your wife back to Nashville, but in the meantime, take up a rail from behind the train. That way we can keep on after them."

"Good idea," Rindell said. "Get started on it." Then he turned toward the farmer. "We thank you, sir, for stopping us. Unfortunately, there will still be a missing rail when we move on. Would you be so kind as to flag down any other train that passes by?"

The farmer nodded. "Like I said, be they Yank or Reb, I don't cotton to killin' folks ridin' on a train."

As the men hurried to move the rail, Rindell climbed the pole to send a wire back to Nashville, explaining the situation. By the time he had completed his message, the rail was in place, and he slid back down the pole and jumped onto the engine, even as it began to roll.

Meanwhile, on the Gold Train, Blackie Chambers had climbed onto the top of the engine tender and was searching the track behind. The instant he saw smoke on the horizon, he knew that they were being pursued. Hurrying, he scrambled back down to the engine.

"Harris! Get this thing going faster! They're coming after us!"

"I'm goin' as fast as I can," Harris said.

"Blackie!" Gerald Ferguson exclaimed. "Get one or two soldiers to help you drop off a car back there. That will slow them down!"

Chambers smiled broadly. He climbed back onto the tender. From there, he reached the top of the first car, then ran the length of the train, jumping the gap from car to car until he finally reached the last boxcar. After climbing down the ladder, he entered the car and recruited two soldiers to come out and pull the connector pin from their car. The task was a dangerous one, especially with the flat wheels causing the train to rock unpredictably, but the pair was successful after a few tries. With both soldiers safely on the forward car's platform with Chambers, the three men watched the detached boxcar begin to drop away immediately, because of its nearly flat wheels and poorly lubricated bearings, while the train continued on.

The two soldiers following him, Chambers crawled back up onto the next car and started his return to the front of the train. At each new car he ordered the two men to climb down to the platform of the forward car, turn around, and pull the connector pin, leaving the rear car behind. Each car had four or five soldiers inside, but that made no difference to Chambers; he assured the two soldiers helping him that their comrades inside the detached boxcars would be rescued soon by a following train.

The process took nearly half an hour, since the operation was extremely hazardous. When they finally reached the first car, Chambers left it attached, instructing the two soldiers to stand guard on its rear platform. It was the car Julia Mayhew was in.

With just one car now connected to the train, Harris was able to gain a little speed. Chambers scurried back across the tender and dropped down onto the engine platform, panting from his effort.

"Let them have the cars with square wheels for awhile and see how fast they can go," he said.

"They're scattering cars along the track!" the engineer shouted to Rindell. "We're going to have to stop for them."

"Can you just pick them up and push them in front of us?" Rindell asked.

"Yes, but we'll have to stop each time to make the connection. We'll lose several minutes on the train up ahead."

"We don't have any choice," Rindell said. "Slow down, so we can hook up to this first car."

As the *Union* approached the stranded boxcar, the four Rebel soldiers who had been inside jumped out and fired one volley. Before they could reload for a second volley, however, the *Union* was right on top of them, and half a dozen of Rindell's men were rushing toward them. The Rebels, seeing that their position was hopeless, threw their arms up in surrender.

"Get them in the car under guard!" Rindell called. "Some of you men, get up on this new car we picked up. You can fire at the Rebels as we approach them!"

The soldiers who had jumped down from the train to rush the defenders of the abandoned boxcar now climbed onto the top of that same car as the *Union* started out in chase again. Rindell left the engine and crawled out to the front of the car with them, to be closer to the Gold Train.

As the *Union* approached the next car, the Rebels who were defending it jumped down and ran away. When the occupants of the third car, only about a hundred yards farther down the track, saw what was happening, they, too, left the fight.

Now the *Union* was pushing three cars before it, and Mike Rindell and the others had moved to the front of the first car. Though these were the same, flat-wheeled cars the Gold Train had been pulling, the engineer driving the *Union* made no effort to slow down, and once again he began closing the distance between his engine and the Gold Train in front of him. Rindell and the soldiers who were riding with him were paying the penalty, though, because the car clattered and clanged and jerked about so that it was difficult to maintain their precarious perch atop it.

On board the Gold Train, Ferguson and Chambers realized that they were being overtaken. The situation seemed desperate until Chambers saw that they were approaching a bridge.

"Dingus!" he shouted to the soldier they had brought forward to replace the fireman when he was killed. "Get some fire out of the firebox and set the car behind us on fire! We'll leave it in the middle of the bridge!"

"Major," Dingus said, looking stunned. "You sure you want to do that?"

"Are you questioning my orders, soldier?"

"No, sir. It's just that . . . well, what about the people in the car?" Dingus asked. "Clark and Bailey are in there. So's the lady."

"Don't concern yourself with them," Chambers snapped.

"Major, I ain't gonna set fire to a car with our own people in it," Dingus said.

"Damn your hide! I gave you an order!" Chambers said. He raised his pistol up and tried to bring it down sharply on the soldier's head, but he underestimated the man's strength. Dingus reached up and caught his arm, then began applying pressure to Chambers's wrist.

"Gerald!" Chambers called, his voice tainted with pain.

Ferguson shot Dingus at point-blank range. The wounded soldier surprised them both when he turned toward Ferguson and with a mighty roar started toward him. Ferguson shot again, and then again.

Dingus had been working without a shirt and now three ugly holes on his bare chest were oozing blood. The last shot had stopped his charge, and now a fourth shot dropped him. Using his foot, Chambers shoved him off the train.

"Damn," Ferguson said. "I was beginning to wonder what it was going to take to stop that big son of a bitch."

Chambers climbed up onto the tender, then traveled the length of the car to where the two soldiers stood guard at the rear. Ordering them to the front of the car, he walked back toward the tender and called to the engineer, "Hand me a shovelful of coals. I'll take care of this myself."

While the engineer carried out his order, Chambers instructed the two soldiers to pull the coupler pin on the boxcar so that it would separate from the engine on the bridge. The two men looked at each other with concern but then began to carry out the dangerous task as ordered. By now the engineer had taken a scoop of coals from the firebox and was handing it up to the major. As the two soldiers worked to separate the remaining boxcar, Chambers took the shovel of coals, hurried across the tender, and scattered them on top of the boxcar. Once he had done the same with a second shovelful, the car was burning, though the two soldiers were unaware of that, so intent were they on the hazardous task they were performing. As the train came onto the bridge, one of the men pulled the coupler pin, dropping the car.

Immediately Chambers yelled, "Jump onto the boxcar! *Now!*"

The two reacted as they had been trained to do. Not questioning the major, they leaped the short gap onto the platform of the boxcar as it moved over the trestle bridge. Neither man was aware that the car was on fire.

The boxcar coasted to a stop right in the middle of the bridge, and as the engine scooted across to the other side, Chambers saw that the top of the car was now blazing furiously.

"That'll stop them!" he shouted as he climbed back into the engine with Ferguson. "They'll have to get Julia out of there, and then they'll have to wait for the car to burn down. By that time, we'll be far, far away."

Once the burning boxcar had come to a stop, the two soldiers on the front platform realized the car was on fire. Gauging the length of the trestle bridge and fearing that the flames would weaken it before they could cross to either side, the two men jumped into the river below.

Inside the burning car, Sergeant Clark and the other guard pushed open the rear door and looked down toward the river below the bridge. Realizing that their best chance for survival was to jump into the water and be carried away before the burning car fell on top of them, the two men called to their prisoner, "Miz Mayhew, come on! We got to jump!"

"I can't!" Julia wailed. "I'm frightened!"

Clark turned to the other guard and said, "Go ahead and get out of here! I'll take care of her."

Taking one quick look, the guard leaped out of the car and into the water, thirty feet below.

"Come on!" Clark yelled, reaching for Julia. "I'll hold on to you on the way down!"

"No . . . I can't!" Julia screamed.

Clark started toward her, but at that moment a burning brand fell from the top of the car, knocking him through the door and down into the river below.

Julia was now alone inside the furiously burning car.

"There's no time to stop and hook the car up!" Rindell shouted, running back to the engineer as they approached the burning car. "Just slow down a bit and push it across the bridge!"

"All right!" the engineer yelled back to him, and complying, he began pushing the burning car. The train managed to push the car to the other side of the bridge without catching the wooden structure on fire, but by the time they reached solid ground, the car Rindell and the soldiers were on was also burning.

"Get off the car!" Rindell ordered, and his men started to abandon their position. That was when Rindell heard a high-pitched scream.

"Help me! Oh, please, someone help me!" Julia Mayhew yelled from inside the blazing car.

"Cap'n! The general's wife! She's still on that car!" Booker shouted.

Rindell jumped onto the roof of the burning car, then swung down inside. Flames were leaping up from all over, and the inside was so thick with smoke he could hardly see.

"Mrs. Mayhew!" he called. "Where are you?"

"Here!" Julia answered, coughing. "Hurry, please, hurry! I can't get out!"

Waving his hands in front of him to fight the smoke, Rindell finally spotted Julia Mayhew. She was lying on the floor, coughing. He quickly moved to her, picked her up, and threw her over his shoulder. Carrying her to the rear door, he jumped across to the platform of the next car, which also was burning, though not quite as badly invested. Once there, he pulled himself up the ladder, with Julia still flung over his shoulder. It was safer to run across the top of the car than to enter the smoke-filled chamber below. Finally, he made it back to the locomotive, where he handed Julia to a couple of the other soldiers. After that, he and another man set to work at pulling the connector pin. When they had succeeded, they signaled for the engineer to back the *Union* up.

The engineer backed up about fifty yards, then stopped, and Rindell climbed down onto the ground beside the track. He stood there, his face blackened with smoke, and watched the two cars burn in front of him.

"Damn!" he swore, hitting his hand against the side of the engine. "There's nothing we can do except sit here and watch them burn!"

Far down the track, he could see the smoke from the stack of the Gold Train, and he heard the whistle blow. He knew it was Chambers, gloating over his escape.

Leah came up to stand beside him.

"How's the woman?" Rindell asked.

"She's going to be all right," Leah said. "Mike, how long do you think it'll take for the cars to burn down enough for us to get them off the track?" she asked.

"A couple of hours, anyway," Rindell replied. He unfolded a map he had taken from MacAphee's office and began examining it. Booker was looking over his shoulder. "I've got to find us another route."

"Cap'n, what if we back up to Pulaski, then take the Huntsville spur? Once we reach Huntsville, we can take this branch back to the main line. That would take us about an hour, but we'd be on the other side of the burning cars."

"Yeah, and Chambers and Ferguson would get an hour's head start," Rindell said.

"It's better than waiting here for another two or three hours."

"You're right," Rindell said. "And I guess the route you suggested is about the best choice." As he started to fold up the map, a quick gust of wind blew in, jerking the paper from his hand. Booker chased after the map, then brought it back. As he did, Rindell turned to look back at the balloon. "Leah, can you make that thing come down anywhere you want?" he asked.

"The balloon? Sure. I can't make it go anywhere I want, but I can make it come down."

"I mean right straight down," Rindell asked.

"Just about," Leah replied. "All you have to do is jerk the rip panel completely off. All the gas escapes and the balloon billows out in the wind. That's called a parachute. Balloonists used to do it at fairs to give people a thrill."

"Yes, well, we're going to give Chambers and Ferguson a thrill," Rindell said. "Right now, the wind is coming out of the northwest. He pointed to the map. The track they're on starts west, then curves back to the southeast. If we go aloft, we'll be blown right over them."

"Either that, or right smack in the middle of the Rebel lines," Leah replied.

"It's the only chance we have of getting the gold back," Rindell said. "Show me what to do, and I—"

"Oh, no," Leah interrupted. "Not on your life, Mike Rindell. You aren't leaving me behind."

Rindell grinned broadly. "Sergeant Booker . . ."

"Cap'n, this here's the Yankee army. I don't reckon I am a sergeant any more," Booker said.

"Well, whatever you are, Booker, hurry up and get that balloon inflated. This chase is about to take to the air."

Booker hurried back to the flatcar, where the gas generator was activated. Because the balloon was already partially inflated, the entire process took less than half an hour. Then, with the balloon tied down to the train, Rindell and Leah climbed into the gondola and released the lines. Without the restraint of the tether line, the balloon rose very quickly, and Rindell soon saw that the *Union* was way below and quite some distance behind them. As he had anticipated, the wind was carrying them southeast, the exact direction he needed to travel in order to intercept the Gold Train.

"There it is!" Leah said, pointing. Several strands of her long black hair had come loose from the chignon into which she had pinned it and were flying in the breeze.

Rindell looked over the edge of the basket. The Gold Train was now just one engine and tender. Free of any cars whatever, it was making very good time.

From this perspective, Rindell could see firsthand what the map had depicted. The track the Gold Train was on bowed slightly to the west and then snaked back to the east. According to the map, it would continue in that direction for another ten miles or so before turning sharply south. Once the train reached that point, balloon pursuit would be impossible, for the balloon was moving southeast.

"There," Rindell said, pointing to a bridge about three miles ahead of the train. "We've got to reach that bridge before the train does. Can we make it?"

"Yes," Leah said. "But perhaps we'd better go down a little. If we go too high, the drift may carry us too far."

Leah vented some of the gas, and the balloon descended slightly. Rindell was just looking over the edge of the basket's rim when he happened to see Confederate soldiers below, discharging a cannon. Something black came hurtling up toward them, and then, about two hundred feet below the balloon, the black object, an explosive cannon shell, burst with a flash of light and a puff of smoke. The sound of the bursting shell and the original sound of the cannon fire reached his ears at about the same time.

"They're shooting cannon at us!" Rindell said. "Don't come down any lower until you have to!"

"All right," Leah agreed.

Two more cannon joined the first, and Rindell watched the shells come hurtling up from the ground. From this perspective the scene was so fascinating that, for the moment, he could almost forget he was their target. Finally he saw that the Gold Train had nearly reached the point where the tracks swung back to the south. He saw, also, that they had overtaken the train and were now in front of it.

"There!" Rindell called. "Can you land us there?"

"Here we go," Leah replied, and she jerked the rip panel open all the way. The gas flowed out of the balloon in a loud hiss as it was replaced by air. The balloon flared out like a giant umbrella, then started down in a rapid, though controlled descent. "Hold on!" Leah called. "We're about to hit the ground!"

Though this landing was much rougher than the first had been, it was not so severe as to cause injury. The basket hit and turned over, spilling Rindell and Leah onto the ground on top of each other. For a moment they were still, and then Rindell pushed himself up and stared at Leah, whose deep blue eyes gazed back at him.

"Are you all right?" Rindell asked with a shy smile.

"Yes," Leah answered. She quickly disentangled herself from him, and both stood up.

Rindell spent a moment brushing off his clothing and then looked around them into the distance. Pointing to a bridge that crossed a gulley, he said, "The Gold Train will be crossing that bridge in another couple of minutes."

"Come on! Let's get up there," Leah suggested.

Moving quickly, they ran across the field, then climbed onto the overhead beams of the bridge. By the time the train rounded the last curve, they were hiding near the top. Rindell looked over at Leah and saw that she was ready.

The train came onto the bridge, the smokestack billowing soot and ash. Rindell waited until the engine had cleared below them, and then he shouted, "Now!"

Both Rindell and Leah dropped down onto the tender car. When he looked into the engine cab, Rindell saw that Gerald Ferguson was stoking the fire, the engineer was driving, and Blackie Chambers was looking out over the field at the balloon, no doubt wondering what it was. Chambers had a pistol in his hand.

"Hello, Blackie," Rindell called.

"What the hell!" Chambers shouted, and he swung his pistol toward Rindell and fired. The bullet hit the top edge of the tender and whistled past Rindell's ear, peppering his face with bits of lead shaved by its impact.

Rindell had his own pistol drawn as well, and he returned fire, his bullet better placed than Chambers's had been. Chambers's gun dropped to the iron deck with a clatter, and the major reached up to grab the wound in his throat. Blood spilled through his hands as he sank to his knees, then fell backward off the train.

Almost immediately upon the heels of Rindell's shot, Ferguson, who had been stoking the furnace, tossed a shovelful of hot coals at Rindell. To protect his eyes, Rindell involuntarily dropped his gun and covered his face with his hands. That action gave Ferguson the opportunity he needed, and he drew his pistol.

Just as Ferguson fired his first shot, Leah jumped down onto the engine deck and grabbed the gun Chambers had dropped. Ferguson's first shot missed its target, because Rindell, even as he was covering his face with his hands, was ducking out of the way. Ferguson's preoccupation with Rindell gave Leah the opening she needed, and she cocked the pistol, aiming it at the turncoat captain.

"Drop your gun!" she shouted to him.

Swinging his pistol toward Leah, Ferguson thumbed back the hammer. Leah watched the cylinder rotating, and though she had hoped he would surrender, she did not hesitate to pull the trigger. She felt the gun discharge in her hand, then saw the look of surprise on Ferguson's face as her bullet crashed into his heart. He fell against the open furnace, then flopped facedown onto the deck.

"That was for Sarah Cunningham," Leah said quietly.

By then, Rindell was up and over the side of the tender car, his own pistol in his hand. He looked at the engineer.

"Are you with them?" he asked.

"Captain, I haven't been with them from the very beginning," he answered. "This young lady will tell you that."

"That's true," Leah said.

"All right, then stop this thing and let's go back to the other train," Rindell said. "We're going to Nashville."

"Yes, sir!" The engineer smiled broadly as he reached for the Johnson bar.

The next morning Mike Rindell and Leah Saunders were standing on the platform at the Nashville depot with Julia Mayhew. She was just about to board the train that would take her to join her husband in Little Rock. Though her eyes were still red from the effects of the smoke from the fire, she was otherwise none the worse for her adventure.

"You're sure you are all right, Mrs. Mayhew?" Leah asked.

Julia Mayhew smiled warmly and replied, "For heaven's sake, Leah, please call me Julia."

"I don't know, that seems a bit presumptuous for a maid, don't you think?" Leah teased.

Julia blushed. "I hope you find it in your heart to forgive me for the awful way I acted on the way out here," she said. "I was such a fool to treat you that way."

"You didn't know who I was," Leah said.

"All the more reason I was a fool," Julia replied, "for I was being harsh and brutal to someone I considered my inferior." She was silent for a moment. "The truth is, no one is my inferior. I have a lot to be thankful for, Leah. Not the least of which is the fortune of meeting the two of you . . ." She paused. "Though you might not understand it, I also feel blessed by meeting Colonel Tyreen. He was truly what they mean when they talk about Southern gentlemen."

"I understand," Rindell said. "Like you, I think Colonel Tyreen was one of the finest gentlemen I ever knew."

The train whistle gave two short blasts, and then General Mayhew's aide-de-camp, a major, came over to speak to Julia.

"Mrs. Mayhew, we'd better get on the train now," he said.

"I'll be right with you, Major," Julia replied. Leah noticed that even the tone of her voice had changed. It was no longer demanding but was now quite pleasant. As the major turned to walk back to the train, Julia looked at Rindell and Leah with a mischievous smile on her face. "I thought aides-de-camp were supposed to be young and handsome." She laughed and then added, "Oh, well, perhaps this is better after all!" She turned and walked away beside the major.

Leah and Rindell laughed as they watched Julia Mayhew and the major disappear into the crowd. Then, realizing that it was nearing their departure time, they walked the full length of the platform to board their train, which Colonel McAphee had arranged to be put together especially to take them back to Washington. It consisted of the engine *Union*, a kitchen car, and the special car that had been put on for Julia's use on the way out.

Colonel MacAphee was waiting for them near the passenger car's platform. He walked up to Rindell and Leah and, putting his arms around their shoulders, said, "I want to thank you two for taking the personal responsibility of returning that car to Washington."

"Consider it our pleasure, Colonel," Rindell replied. "We're delighted to be returning the car for you." He smiled and put his thumbs on the lapels of his forest-green jacket. "But if you will notice my clothes, Colonel, you will see that I am no longer a captain."

"No," MacAphee said. "I guess not. Though you performed so admirably in that capacity that I'm sure I could secure a permanent commission for you if you wanted one."

"Ah, thank you, no," Rindell said. "I'm afraid Mr. Faraday wouldn't be too pleased with that."

"Well, if you ever change your mind, just let me know." MacAphee stuck out his hand and shook first Rindell's hand, then Leah's. "It's been nice knowing the two of you, and I hope you have a pleasant trip back."

Rindell and Leah watched MacAphee as he walked away. Then Leah turned her blue eyes up toward Rindell and smiled. "And will we?" she asked.

"Will we what?"

"Have a pleasant trip back?"

"What do you think?" he replied. He put his thumb and forefinger under Leah's chin and turned her face up toward his. Then he kissed her, long and slow, oblivious to the tramping of booted feet as a platoon of soldiers marched by.

"Hey, Cap'n, what're you doin'?"

"Ebenezer, you ain't got any more sense in this army than you did in the other'n," Booker snapped. Booker, a private now, was in the ranks, marching alongside his friend, both of them in the new blue uniforms of the Union Army. "Don't pay no attention to him, Cap'n. You just go right on a doin' what you was doin'."

With his arms still around Leah, Mike Rindell looked over at the platoon of men and smiled.

"Oh, I intend to, Booker. I intend to," he said. "All the way back to Washington."

Watch for

THE COLORADO SPECIAL

next in the Faraday series
coming soon from
Lynx Books!